Let Love
Rescue Ya

Deborah Thayer
McLane

Rescued

by

Love

DEBORAH THAYER MCLAIN

WESTBOW
PRESS®
A DIVISION OF THOMAS NELSON
& ZONDERVAN

WestBow Press books may be ordered through booksellers or by contacting:

WestBow Press
A Division of Thomas Nelson & Zondervan
1663 Liberty Drive
Bloomington, IN 47403
www.westbowpress.com
1 (866) 928-1240

ISBN: 978-1-9736-2602-2 (sc)
ISBN: 978-1-9736-2603-9 (hc)
ISBN: 978-1-9736-2601-5 (e)

Library of Congress Control Number: 2018904517

Print information available on the last page.

WestBow Press rev. date: 04/18/2018

God rescued us from dead-end alleys and dark dungeons. He's set us up in the kingdom of the Son he loves so much, the Son who got us out of the pit we were in, got rid of the sins we were doomed to keep repeating.

Colossians 1:13-14 MSG

Contents

Foreword

A couple of years ago, Deborah came to me and our friend, Karen, to tell us about this story that was spinning around in her head. She was so excited about it, and her excitement was infectious. I found myself following every word she said. She knew she wanted to write it all down but wasn't even thinking of getting it published. As the months went by, she kept me, and Karen updated on what she was writing and how far along she was. She even uploaded and shared her progress with us. I had read a couple of pages in the beginning, but soon life got in the way, and I lost track.

Fast forward to the end of 2017. Deborah had finished her story. We had been talking about her story in small increments over the years and how maybe she would like to get it published someday. One day after church, we were talking like we usually did after the service, and she nonchalantly told me she was looking for publishers and came across this website. As she talked, a huge smile crept across her face and stayed there. It seemed that she had made up her mind to get it published after all. She asked me to read a part that was integral to the story. I got caught up in it and tears started to stream down my face. It was one of the most beautiful things I had ever read.

Pieces just seemed to fall into place for her. She talked with a few people at the publishers who loved the concept. There were a couple of bumps in the road, but through it all, she put her faith in God to get it done. I was amazed as I watched her through the whole process. When things went wrong or not the way she had expected them to go, she was cool under pressure and full of grace. She trusted God because she knew that He gave her this story to write.

I am honored and privileged that she trusted me to help her edit this story that God has placed in her heart. As you read this book, please remember how much God loves and cherishes his church. Most of all, know how much he loves you, how he has fought for you and ultimately paid the price for you.

I hope you enjoy it and maybe guess which part I cried at.

Lauren

Acknowledgment

To the most encouraging editor I know, Lauren Wicke. I am so grateful for our friendship that has grown because of this book.

To my husband who encouraged me along the way and never grew tired of my "book" conversations.

To friends like Karen Mejeur and Donna Cody who always cheered me on.

Dia Richoet

Dia Richoet was a grand castle built into the sides of rocky cliffs high above the open ocean. Many villagers called this castle the defiant stronghold. Long ago, villagers had stayed within the castle walls for protection against a great storm. Although the storm washed away many homes in the surrounding villages, the castle stood unshaken, and all who sought refuge within the walls remained safe. The castle stubbornly refused to obey the commands of the strong winds and crashing waves.

Sitting tall and proud on his royal steed, Cullen watched the waves crash against the cliffs. Cullen spent many days preparing for battle. His subjects knew him as a mighty warrior ready to fight for and protect his people. His dark, straight hair was carefully trimmed to his shoulders. His eyes were his most captivating feature. Many people said that they looked like the crystal-blue water of the springs of Cura. The peace that filled his soul seemed to flow out of his eyes. Just being around him gave many people a sense of peace.

Even though he had great tranquility, something had been on his mind recently. He had been experiencing very vivid dreams, dreams he could not explain. Cullen needed to clear his mind, and he knew just the way—an afternoon ride on his horse, Hunter. Hunter was a feisty, spirited horse. Under Cullen's firm hand, he became a gentle horse, extremely loyal to Cullen. His black mane, tail, and socks accented his light-tan coat. Hunter's ability to run, and jump well made him a favorite at festivals and Cullen admired Hunter's strength and speed. On this early spring day, the chill in the air would help keep Hunter cool for a long run.

Cullen loved the vastness and variety of the landscape in his kingdom. He enjoyed taking in the majestic beauty, strength, and power of the ocean. Near the castle, trees grew twisted and tilted as they obeyed the wind's command. Cullen looked beyond Dia Richoet. There, protected from the strong winds, the landscape took on a slightly different appearance. Instead of the twisted trees, there were lush fields of wildflowers gently blowing in the breeze. Children laughed gleefully as they ran through the flowers. Elsewhere, farmers worked the ground tirelessly, plowing and planting their fields with wheat in hopes of an abundant harvest

Cullen set his mind to the east where his father's kingdom awaited his return. Cullen longed to revisit his father but knew he still had a lot to do before he could return home. One could quickly travel on horseback and reach the rolling hills of the east. Rich green pastures dotted the landscape, and ancient stone walls drew lines across the grassy slopes.

The farther one traveled into the rolling hills, the steeper they became. The heavy spring dew watered the grass, and excellent pastures were plentiful. However, because of the steep hills, only the younger, healthy sheep could graze those tender grasses. The older sheep would have to settle for the lower pastures that were also very green, especially along the gently flowing rivers.

To the south of Dia Richoet stood Cullen's only enemy, King Dorcha. Ruling Chrioch Olc, King Dorcha became widely known for his brutality. Cullen knew he always needed to stay alert, watching for any activity from King Dorcha. However, a vast, dense forest grew between Chrioch Olc and Dia Richoet making it difficult for any army to organize an attack. Sometimes the dense fog hung so low and thick that one could barely see a few feet in front of him. Some believed evil creatures remained hidden in the trees. Despite its gloomy appearance, Cullen knew the most serious trouble was the fog. Any good soldier could easily get lost and lose his sense of direction.

Looking to the north, Cullen could envision the steep, rugged mountains. Mormhuir Cathair, a peaceful country ruled by his friend King Luke, was located on the other side of the mountain range. The journey to Mormhuir Cathair was dangerous and took several days traveling by horseback, going by foot could prove deadly. Mormhuir Cathairs' countryside was similar to Dia Richoet, except plentiful beaches with gently rolling waves replaced the cliffs abutting the ocean. Easy access to the sea made Mormhuir Cathair a vital trade route. Merchants traveled far distances to trade their goods in one of the many bustling seaport villages.

Keela

Keela woke with a start and jumped out of bed. She could barely contain her excitement. As she rushed to the window to pull the curtains away, she smiled. *Perfect,* she thought. *The sun is shining brightly on this glorious day.* She had known for several years that on her eighteenth birthday, her gift would be her freedom.

For as long as Keela could remember, this had been her home. The nuns had raised her in this convent since she was a young child. She knew that the sisters loved her deeply, but she always wondered who her birth parents were. Why did they leave her here in the nuns' custody? What had she done wrong in her young life to cause her parents to desert her in this place? After the day of celebration, with teary goodbyes and lots of hugs, Keela left the only family she knew.

She stood there with the convent behind her, and the road that symbolized her freedom stretched out before her. As she began down the long path with great anticipation, she thought, *How am I going to find a place to sleep tonight? I don't have any money, and I have never worked before.* She began to feel concerned. *I don't want to spend the night out in the wilderness! No, I am not going to worry about those kinds of things yet. It will all work out.*

Her determination returned as she continued down the long, straight road that led to the village. In the far distance, a small outcropping of woods lined the horizon. All her life she had looked at the trees and wondered what life must be like in the village.

5

Keela enjoyed the sweet fragrances of the beautiful wildflowers that lined the road, and the warmth of the sun as it shone brightly. She loved the springtime. Everything about spring brought her enjoyment. It felt like things were starting over with the trees budding and the flowers blooming. She breathed in deeply as she continued her walk. This new sense of freedom wasn't so scary now. At least with the sun shining, everything seemed to be all right.

As she neared the trees, she realized that what from a distance appeared to be a small grove was more like a vast forest. Keela remembered some of the stories she had heard of the wild animals that lived in the woods and the robbers who would lie in wait for a passing traveler. Keela began to feel anxious. *Well, I don't have any money, so if a robber comes by, I will explain to them that I have no money and I don't come from a wealthy family. I doubt they will bother me.* She hoped that she would not see any of the wild animals.

Wrapping her shawl a little tighter around her shoulders to ward off the chill, she continued down the wooded path into the forest. She noticed that the smells were very different. She breathed in the aroma of fresh pine. Looking up at the tall trees she thought, *I wonder what it must be like to look out from the top of those tall pine trees. It must be an incredible sight to see. I wish I were a bird so I could fly high and see what lies ahead. What does the sunset look like from such a height?* As she walked deeper into the forest, the thick plant growth surprised her. Bushes and ferns covered the forest floor.

She grew hungry and noticed that the sun was slowly sinking in the sky. She thought, *I hope I finish walking through the forest before dusk. I don't want to have to find shelter in the woods.* She sat down on a flat stone and pulled out a small piece of bread from her bag. The nuns had given her a little food, but she had no idea when she would have her next meal, so she ate as little as possible. As she ate, she heard a rustle in the bushes. Fear gripped her heart. *Sit perfectly still—maybe it won't see me.* Just then, a gentle doe and her young fawn came into view. Keela watched these beautiful creatures as they grazed on the flowering bushes. *Are these the wild animals people warned me about? They are not scary.* Peace started taking over her heart. Perhaps there was nothing to fear. She would find a place to sleep safely tonight. She just knew it.

After her small dinner and a brief rest, she continued toward the village. In the path just ahead, she saw two men walking toward her. She steeled herself against the fear that began to creep into her heart and tried her best to remain calm. She would walk straight toward them and politely walk around them as she headed to the village. *They are probably two harmless villagers,* she tried convincing herself. Instead of remaining calm, her heart began to race. Both men continued to walk directly toward her. The closer they came, the more she became determined to just walk past them.

"Hello. Beautiful day for a walk, isn't it?"

The two men stood directly in front of her without saying a word.

"Excuse me," Keela said, trying not to show that she was getting nervous.

Instead of stepping aside, they stood side by side blocking the path and would not let her pass.

"We've been waiting a long time to watch you come down that path," one of them growled.

"Finally, the king will reward us for catching you. He's been wanting to talk to you for quite some time," grumbled the other man.

"What are you talking about? Please, I am not the person you think I am. I don't know anyone in the village. Let me pass!" Keela pleaded.

"We'll let King Luke decide about that," the first man said as he took her by the arm. "Come with us."

"Where are you taking me?"

"I just told you. King Luke wants to see you."

Keela was confused she didn't know where they were taking her or who King Luke was. "Please. I don't even know where I am! What is the name of King Luke's domain?"

The second man looked at her in disbelief. "You're in Mormhuir Cathair, of course."

"That's enough questions!" The first man shouted. He glared at the other man as if to say too much was said.

Keela did not argue but allowed the men to take her with them. She found a little comfort in knowing she would no longer be alone in the woods. Soon, she would be in the presence of a king. She hoped he would have mercy on her after she explained the mistake of these men.

Dreams

Marcus had been close friends with Cullen since they were old enough to walk. Over the years Cullen had watched his friend become an excellent warrior. He was significantly shorter than most of his men, and what he lacked in height, he made up for in strength. Marcus was brave and valiant and would lay his life down for his king. He had deep brown eyes and wavy dark brown hair. His confident smile would cheer up an entire room. Cullen had recently promoted Marcus to be the captain of his army. Cullen's men loved serving under Marcus because they knew he cared about each one of them individually. They were all treated like family. He understood authority and performed all his work with deep confidence.

Marcus had become a confidant for Cullen. He would quietly sit and listen as Cullen shared the burdens of his heart. Marcus had never once betrayed that trust. Now, Cullen wanted to speak with Marcus as a friend. Recently, he had been experiencing a lot of puzzling dreams that he could not explain. Cullen knew he could confide in Marcus. They had read and studied the legend since they were young boys. The tale spoke about a king and queen who could communicate through dreams. Through pure love and sacrifices, they would overcome death and change the entire Kingdom. The whole empire would have many generations of peace.

Could I possibly be living that legend? Cullen wondered, *I need to*

talk this over with Marcus. He will help me sort through my thoughts.
Cullen summoned for Marcus.

Marcus entered the room quickly, "You called me, my lord?"

"Yes, Marcus. I have a lot on my mind. Can we talk?" Cullen motioned toward a seat.

"Of course, my lord. What is it?" Marcus' expression held a look of concern as he took a seat across from Cullen.

"Please stop calling me 'my lord'. Right now, I just want a friend," Cullen smiled.

Marcus looked relieved, "Yes, sir." Marcus leaned forward in his seat.

"Marcus, do you remember when we were younger, and we studied the legend?"

"Yes," Marcus could not hide his look of surprise.

Cullen continued, "I am sure you weren't expecting me to be talking about the legend. Did you ever really think it might happen to us?"

Marcus turned slightly in his seat to study the look on Cullen's face. "Cullen, you know I always hoped it was true. The legend states that when the king finds his bride and marries her, many generations will experience peace. They would have destroyed all their enemies and peace would reign across the entire domain."

Cullen looked frustrated. "The legend also states that the king and queen can hear and communicate to each other without speaking. Some people believe that they will be able to talk to each other in their mind. You and I know that's not possible … right?"

Marcus stifled a chuckle, "yes. I agree, but …" Marcus hesitated to finish his thought.

"But what?"

"It is called a legend because it seems there is no truth in it. If it were common, people would not recognize it, and anyone could say they were part of the legend."

Cullen leaned back in his chair and looked up at the ceiling. "Yes, I thought of that too, but how would the villagers know?"

Curiously Marcus said. "My lord, forgive me for prying, but why are you questioning the legend? Do you hear voices?"

Cullen seemed a little apprehensive, "I know it sounds crazy, but yes. At night, I can hear a woman faintly crying. She is scared, lonely and confused."

For a moment, neither of them said a word.

Cullen looked at his friend. "Do you think I am crazy? I mean, what if It's just some strange dream?"

"How long has this dream been happening?"

"Only for a few weeks now. It's just at night; her voice is so quiet I can barely hear it."

"Cullen, I don't know what to tell you. Perhaps if you traveled a little in the kingdom, you would hear her louder, clearer, or maybe you would not hear her at all."

Cullen sat a little straighter in his chair. "Why would you suggest that?"

Marcus continued, "Well if you traveled in a direction and her voice got louder, you would know that you were getting closer to her. Maybe she's just too far away, and you really can't hear her," Marcus said.

"So, you mean to tell me that you think perhaps I am living the legend? I am not losing my mind. Do you think this legend could be true?"

"Perhaps, my lord, but you won't know until you try to find her."

Moria

Years ago, Marcus had been injured in battle. It was not a life-threatening injury, but a difficult one nonetheless. An arrow pierced through the leather in his armor and lodged itself deep into his shoulder. One of his men went to fetch the doctor while Marcus waited in his house. When the local doctor arrived, a beautiful young woman walked in with him. Women were rarely seen helping the doctor for any medical emergency. Marcus could barely take his eyes off her. She had a very positive spirit. Her eyes sparkled with a genuine smile that lit up her entire face and showed compassion and concern. The doctor noticed Marcus' attraction to his nurse.

"Marcus, let me introduce you to my assistant, Moria. I think she is the most helpful assistant I have ever had. Never mind the prettiest."

Moria blushed when she heard what the doctor said. Marcus thought she looked even more beautiful. The gentle pink that colored her face gave it a softer look.

"Come on, Doc. Now you embarrassed the girl." Marcus enjoyed teasing her but knew that soon when the doctor began to remove the arrow, all joking would be put aside. "Let's get this over with Doc. This arrow is killing me."

Marcus waited a moment, expecting Moria to leave the room, but instead, Marcus heard the doctor give her instruction as to what he expected her to do.

"I will be back shortly, Marcus; Moria will take care of your needs for the moment," the doctor said as he walked out of the room.

Moria turned toward him and smiled. "I know most men don't want a woman around when they are injured." Her eyes held a slight look of sadness. She held Marcus' gaze for a moment, then turning toward a table, she prepared the tools the doctor would need. "My father and brothers were like that. I wanted to become a doctor, but they told me a woman belonged in the home, not as a doctor tending to the wounds of men. They were all too proud to accept my help when they were injured. Moria turned and handed him a glass. "Here, this should help with the pain a little bit. Sorry. I don't know if it will help much. This arrow is lodged in quite far."

Marcus took the glass and swallowed the bitter juice quickly. A few moments after he drank the liquid the doctor stepped back into the room. Marcus wanted to ask her more about what she just said but now was not the time. Instead, he looked at her and said, "Well, I am honored to have you help the doctor. I can tell you care about people." Soon the drink that she gave him began to make his mind cloudy. He felt numb all over.

"Alright," the doctor said, "I can tell by your expression that the medicine is helping. Let's get this over with."

Marcus struggled to remain calm even though the excruciating pain. It took all the strength he could muster not to cry out in pain in front of this beautiful young lady. When Marcus awoke, he heard a quiet rustling in the corner of the room. He slowly turned and saw Moria standing with her back toward him working on something on the table. She seemed to know when he woke up and turned around.

"Well, good morning," she said with a smile.

Being the captain of the army, he had women continually trying to win his attention. This girl didn't seem to be like that at all.

"I must admit, you handled that very well. I don't know how you didn't cry out. I think the medicine practically put you to sleep."

Marcus laughed aloud. "Oh, you don't know the half of it," he chuckled again, "I wanted to cry out. I probably would have if you were not there." He gave her a grin. "It's amazing what happens to an injured man when you put a beautiful lady in the room."

Moria blushed. "My lord, please. I am just an ordinary woman, nothing special."

"Well, I don't agree. You are a remarkable woman. Thank you for your help."

Moria slid a chair up to the side of his bed. "What is your name?" That comment surprised Marcus. Because of his title, he often felt like all the women in the entire kingdom knew his name.

"My name is Marcus. I recently received the position to be the Captain of the army for King Cullen."

Moria looked at him and smiled. "You have a lot of responsibilities. How do you handle it when one of your men dies in battle?"

Marcus thought about her question for a moment. "Well, I haven't lost anyone, yet. However, I know I would be very distraught. Why do you ask?"

Moria's expression saddened, and her eyes had a far-off look. Marcus didn't want to continue to ask if she didn't want to talk, but after a moment of silence, she spoke. "My two brothers died in battle," she said slowly. Marcus could hear the sorrow in her voice.

"I am sorry." Marcus knew he had asked too much, but Moria continued.

"My family lived in King Dorcha's kingdom."

Again, Marcus could feel her sorrow. He had heard many stories from people who were in King Dorcha's army. He was a brutal king and did not regard his people's lives with any worth. "Moria, you must have gone through a lot. I am sorry for prying."

Morias' eyes were watery now. "It's all right," she said with a weak smile, "I needed to talk to someone about it. I wish my brothers served under you, instead. I wanted to help my brothers, but they refused. They wanted to wait for a doctor. I know I could have saved my little brother if he let me help him." The tears began flowing down her face. "I'm sorry," she said as she got up and walked out of the room.

Marcus knew her story was a difficult one; he just didn't realize how hard. What could he say to her to help ease her mind?

Around dinner time, Moria returned with some hot stew. "Well, I guess the doctor wants me to take care of you personally," she said with a smile, "What do you think of that?"

Marcus smiled, "I couldn't be happier. The doctor knows how to get me on my feet quickly."

Moria chuckled, "Don't be so happy. You don't know if I am tough or gentle. I have been told I am a very tough nurse."

"Perhaps, but I believe if you're tough it's because you want to see me moving around faster. I trust you are a good doctor."

Moria looked at him. "You mean nurse," she said curtly.

"I said doctor," Marcus said in a gentle but firm voice, "I believe you will make a great doctor soon."

Moria looked frustrated. "I know you're just trying to be nice, but I will never be allowed to be a doctor. You forget I am a woman, and that's not allowed."

Marcus wasn't giving in that easy. "Maybe with King Dorcha, it's not allowed, but we will see what King Cullen has to say about it. I for one will give you a high recommendation, and the doctor spoke highly of you, as well."

Moria just stared at him. "You mean to tell me that you would talk to the king for me?" Her face showed her shock, yet her voice showed her excitement.

"Of course, I would talk to Cullen for you. I am sure he would be very open to the idea. It's not whether you're a man or woman that would make you a good doctor, it's your compassion for people and your knowledge of how to make them better."

A few years later, Moria had become his wife. Her confident attitude and dedication made her a well-loved doctor in the local village.

Almost found

Keela sat in her dungeon. As hard as she tried, she couldn't make sense of why she was locked up in this cell. Just a few weeks ago she left the convent, and now she is being accused of lying. What did King Luke want with her? He asked her all kinds of questions about a king and a kingdom that she never heard of. His words echoed in her mind. "Your husband is the king. Who are his allies? Your parents gave you a great weapon to destroy your enemies. What is it?"

He kept claiming that she changed her name! Why would she change her name? She had been called Keela her entire life. Occasionally, it would bother her knowing that she could not remember who her parents were, but she did not think that worthy of prison. King Luke did not seem like he enjoyed keeping her prisoner. He just wanted answers. Answers to questions that she could not give. She tried many times to convince him that he had the wrong person. He became slightly angered at her comment, but he never retaliated in any way.

King Luke had heard of a powerful kingdom that would conquer all their enemies and reign in peace for many decades. He explained the legend to Keela and told her how it concerned him. His kingdom had experienced peace for many years, and Luke did not want that to change. His people were peaceful; he knew his army would not be able to stand against a great foe. Keela tried to tell King Luke to become friends with the stronger empire. She explained that his country would have peace when the stronger empire had times of peace. King Luke seemed to like that idea. He thought about it for several minutes.

"You are a wise woman," he said. "However, it doesn't mean you're a free woman. I have been told that you are a queen that will influence that kingdom. Why would I let you go free?"

Keela's eyes were wide with unbelief. "My lord, I am not a queen. I am simply an orphan with no family. However, if you let me free and I end up becoming a queen someday, I will remember your mercy and repay your kindness to you and your people."

King Luke did not respond to that; he had left the room without saying a word. Several days had passed since that conversation. *At least I have a place to sleep, and I have been receiving meals each day,* she thought to herself, *I just went from one prison cell to another.*

Cullen needed answers and needed them fast. If the dreams that he had been having for the past few weeks continued, he would be exhausted from lack of sleep. Cullen wanted to reread the legend, which was stored in an ancient library located several days journey away in a northern village. He gave Marcus authority to run the kingdom on his own while he was away.

The farther Cullen traveled north, the stronger and louder he could hear the voice calling for help. He thought about what Marcus had said earlier. Now that the woman's voice became louder, he decided not to go the ancient library but to look for the woman instead. Whenever the woman called out to him, Cullen could tell that she was scared and confused. Cullen found that after a second day's travel, he could hear her with such clarity, he could almost imagine where she sat and what the room looked like. She was in a cell, He could feel the cold dungeon wall as she leaned against them. It was well lit and not too cold.

As he continued north, he wondered about this woman. *I wonder what her name is, can she hear me? What did she do that deserved being held, prisoner?* Well, tonight he would find out. Cullen would travel as far north as he could before nightfall, find a safe place to build a shelter, and then try to communicate to her.

The farther north he traveled, the more treacherous the terrain became. Looking for either an outcrop of rocks to use as a shelter or a cove of trees for protection, Cullen found a place he could rest for the night. After years of training for battle, he had become an expert archer. He had won many competitions over the years, but he didn't like to hunt unless it became necessary. Tonight, he was thankful for his skill as he enjoyed roasted rabbit he cooked on the open fire.

Cullen tried to focus; he needed to figure out how to communicate with this woman whom he only heard in his sleep. *If I fall asleep, am I going to be able to talk with her?* He drifted off into a fitful sleep. The questions began to fill his mind.

Why am I here?

That voice, so close and loud; it woke him up out of his sleep.

"Hello?" he yelled, "Hello?!? Who is there?" The silence of the forest echoed back in his ears. Cullen realized that the voice belonged to the woman he could hear in his sleep. Again, he drifted back to sleep. *Where are you?* He thought.

Where am I? The woman responded, *How am I supposed to know, I am locked in a dungeon. Interrogated about things I have no understanding of ...* For a moment there was silence: *wait a minute I can't believe I am talking to myself. Great!*

No, you're not talking to yourself; you're talking to me. Cullen thought, *Do you know who is keeping you in the dungeon?*

After several minutes of silence, she said, *King Luke is his name, I can't remember what the country is called... he keeps asking me questions about some legend. That's all I know.*

Silence filled the night and Cullen's' mind. He could no longer communicate with the woman. *Why did that conversation end so abruptly?* He wondered. Cullen decided to travel more in the morning.

Keela woke with a start. The dream was so realistic. *That was so strange! I have never dreamt like that before. It felt so real like I was actually talking with a man,* she thought. Her entire dream centered on who held her captive. Hearing footsteps echoing on the hard-stone floor, she shook her head trying to forget about that strange dream. As she looked up, she saw King Luke himself had come to visit her in the dungeon.

"I've thought a lot about what you said," he started. "I've decided to let you go free. If you are not lying to me, then you do not know the answers to the questions I have asked. Please remember my mercy if you ever become queen."

Relief flooded Keela's mind. "My lord, I don't think it is possible for me to become queen of any kingdom. I am only a beggar. I have no home, no family and no understanding of the kingdom that you seek. Still, I will forever be grateful for your mercy and understanding. Thank you for giving me my freedom, but where am I to go now?"

"You may stay in the village if you would like. I have people who would give you a place to sleep, but you must find a job and your own house within a month. I will also give you a small parcel of land for you to grow food."

"That is most gracious of you, my lord. Thank you."

"Come with me; I will have my maids assist you and provide you with a clean dress and a bath. You will sit with me for dinner. Then I will introduce you to the family who will be taking care of your needs temporarily."

Keela could hardly believe how quickly things had changed. True to his word, King Luke provided her with a clean dress, a feast, and a place to stay. That night, sleeping in a real bed, Keela slept so soundly. She wasn't uncomfortable, and she didn't dream of voices. Tomorrow would be a new day filled with great possibilities.

Cullen traveled north for three more days. Even though he tried each night, he could not hear the woman again. *Why did the dreams suddenly stop?* Cullen thought to himself as he woke from his fitful sleep. Noticing storm clouds on the horizon. He broke down camp and loaded Hunter with his bedding roll; talking to Hunter as he rubbed the horse's shoulders. "Hunter, it looks like we should find some shelter before that storm settles in, Mormhuir Cathair is just a short distance away. Let's go visit my friend Luke. I'm sure he will let us wait out the storm."

Cullen wandered around the seaport of Mormhuir Cathair. *Could the woman be around here somewhere?* He wondered as he mingled with the villagers. He smiled at the children running in the streets, and the old women selling in the marketplace. Cullen breathed in a long deep breath of the salt air mixed with the scents of the busy market.

Soon the rains began to pour. Cullen headed to the castle to seek out his friend, King Luke. Seeing them coming into the courtyard a stable hand greeted them.

"Good day my lord, are you staying for a little while? Would you like me to tend to the needs of your horse?"

Cullen dismounted Hunter. "Yes, please dry him off and let him stay in the stables. I will come get him when I am finished meeting with King Luke. If possible, I may wait out the storm for a few days."

"Yes, sir," said the stable hand.

Cullen turned, walked into the courtyard, and finding a guard, approached him. "Good day. Could you please let King Luke know that King Cullen is here and would like to visit with him?"

"Yes, sir," the guard said as he bowed slightly before Cullen. "Just a moment."

A few minutes later Luke came into the room. "Cullen! What a pleasant surprise! What brings you all the way to Mormhuir Cathair?"

Cullen didn't want to try to explain the dreams to Luke, "Well, I was out making the rounds of my domain when this storm approached. Mormhuir Cathair was closer that Dia Richoet so I was hoping you would allow me to find safe refuge until the storm passed."

Luke's smile spread from ear to ear. "Old friend, I would have it no other way. Is Hunter safely put in the royal stables?"

"Yes, your stable worker already took care of Hunter."

"Good. Come, we have some catching up to do. I haven't seen you for a few years!"

The storm lasted two days, but with all the heavy rains, Cullen knew traveling across the steep mountains would not be safe. Luke allowed him to stay another four days to be sure that the roads would be clear, and travel would be easier.

Disappointed that he did not find or hear from the woman since he arrived in Mormhuir Cathair, Cullen thanked his friend Luke for his hospitality. With his horse loaded with goods that he had purchased from the marketplace, he turned Hunter south to begin his journey back home.

Baby on the way

Marcus walked into the room looking weary and worn out.

"Is something bothering you, Marcus?" Concern marked Cullen's face.

"Well," Marcus let out a deep sigh, "I haven't slept in a few nights, but I am sure that's not what you wanted to talk to me about," Marcus said.

"Marcus, I have lots to talk about for sure. I haven't slept well lately, either. Your life is just as important to me. Tell me what's going on. Why can't you sleep?"

"It's my wife. As you know, she is with child, but her health is failing. I don't know what to do. I can't seem to sleep. I just lay in bed watching her. What if she needed help in the night, and I didn't hear her ask for help? I know the baby is coming soon, but she looks so weak and pale. I am afraid of losing her."

Cullen thought about that for a while. How could he help his friend? Marcus' wife Moria was like life to Marcus. He couldn't understand the fear that Marcus must be dealing with.

Marcus hung his head and took a deep, ragged breath.

"Have you spoken to the doctor about your concern?" Cullen asked.

"Yes, we have spoken."

"What is happening to Moria that makes you afraid she will not make it through childbirth?"

"She is in a lot of pain in her abdomen when she stands. If she tried to get out of bed to make dinner, she begins to sweat profusely and becomes very dizzy. Not to mention she barely eats anything. When she does eat dinner, she normally gets sick later that night. One time, she tried to go for a small walk, but I had to help her home she became too weak to stand. Moria keeps telling me that she's fine, just tired, but she just doesn't look right."

Cullen thought about Moria's neighbors. "Isn't Nancy your neighbor? She's helped many women in the kingdom go through childbirth. I'm sure she could be a great help when the time comes."

"Yes, I have already spoken to her. She has agreed to come any time of day or night. I just need to get her. I guess that's why I haven't been sleeping. I don't want to miss the time Moria says she needs me."

"Marcus, I think you would wake very quickly when Moria calls your name. Did Nancy give you any advice about Moria's health?"

"Nancy thinks I should be trying to feed Moria more meat, and she should be out in the sunshine even taking walks if possible. Moria won't do any of those things. She's afraid that even sitting up in bed will make the baby come early." Marcus looked up at Cullen with eyes that were so deep with sorrow, it practically hurt Cullen to look at him. "Cullen, I couldn't live if something ever happened to her. She's all I live for!"

Cullen tried to console his friend. "You would continue to live, Marcus. Of course, your heart would be breaking, but you would have a child to take care of. I know you would fight for that child with all your heart."

Marcus hung his head to hide the tears that stung his eyes. Yes, he would do everything in his power to take care of his child if Moria died. He just wasn't ready to live without his precious Moria.

Cullen thought, *what can I do to help? Here I am, king of a great kingdom and my hands are tied. How can I help my friend and his wife?* Suddenly he had an idea; he would have the best doctor in his kingdom stay at his castle with Marcus, his wife, and Nancy. That way when the child would be born, all the people that could help would be there. No chance for something to go wrong while they waited for the doctor to arrive.

Marcus thought the idea was perfect. He may even get some sleep knowing that people were attentive to Moria's needs. However, Marcus knew Moria would not agree to it. She had a hard time moving; just getting her out of bed was very difficult. How would he get her to the castle? He tried not to share his thoughts with Cullen; he was only trying to help. When Marcus left, his heart still just as heavy as before, but at least he knew he had a friend and Cullen would do anything he could to help. Marcus knew this was his burden to carry. He could just pray that his precious Moria would be strong enough when the baby came.

Cullen wanted to speak with Marcus about the legend. *I can't bother him about the legend right now, he's got enough on his mind. I will just go to Nochtadh to the ancient library and study the ancient parchment again.*

Mormhuir Cathair

It had been months since King Luke had spoken with Keela, but her words seemed to echo in his mind. Maybe he should take her advice and ask to ally with King Cullen of Dia Richoet. Luke had sent a request to King Cullen to come and talk about the possibilities of becoming allies.

Luke looked out at the busy seaport. His people had experienced peace for many years, but if the legend were right, a war would likely start. The port left him vulnerable to attack by sea. This worried King Luke. If he could become allies with King Cullen, Luke could call on his army for help. He had been envious of Cullen's army and knew he would benefit from that friendship. Luke looked out at the busy seaport. Many fishermen and trading boats came from all distances. *I can offer King Cullen my seaport goods as a trade for his protection,* he thought.

Cullen sat in the throne room tending to the needs and requests of his people when a young messenger boy came into the outer courts. Marcus approached Cullen in the throne room.

"My lord, there is a messenger here to see you."

"Please bring him in," Cullen watched the boy enter the room. He assumed the boy's age to be about ten years old. The boy's eyes were wide with awe as he came into the throne room.

"You have a message for me?"

"Yes, sir," the boy said as he bowed low before Cullen.

"My lord, I bring word from King Luke of Mormhuir Cathair. He requests a visit with you and the captain of your army."

Cullen and Marcus exchanged surprised looks.

"Tell me, son, is King Luke well?"

"Yes, sir. He is fine. I do not know the meaning of his request," the young boy replied.

Cullen noticed that the boy looked anxious as he stood before him. "Did you travel through those mountains alone?"

"Yes sir," the boy said as he stood straight and tall, "I know those mountains very well, sir."

Cullen couldn't help but smile at the boy. "You are a courageous little man."

"Thank you, my lord,"

Cullen continued, "Please ask the stable boy to ready my horse, Marcus, and I will come with you to visit King Luke. Perhaps you can show us an easier way to travel through those steep mountains."

"Yes, sir," the boy said as he bowed low again then turned and left the room.

Cullen turned to Marcus, "I know your wife is close to bearing the child. Do you think we have a few days to take this journey?"

Marcus looked nervous, "Well, the doctor said we still have several weeks or maybe up to a month to wait. I just don't know."

"Marcus, if you would rather stay here, I will take Flanigan with me in your place."

"No, my Lord, I will come. I just hope the doctor is right and Moria understands."

Cullen had made the journey with Marcus and the messenger boy to the kingdom of Mormhuir Cathair. Cullen looked around the seaport. It had only been a few months since he was here seeking shelter from a storm. Now it was late fall. The marketplace appeared very different. The fish and the fresh vegetables were unlike the market sold in the summer. Women were selling their warm hand woven goods, instead of light woven baskets. As requested, Cullen and Marcus went directly to the castle to see Luke. As Cullen and King Luke spoke, Luke offered Cullen the trade of the seaport and the fisheries in his country for his protection, should an attack ever come by sea.

"A wise woman had once told me to seek allies with my neighbors," Luke continued, "I am not expecting war; I am just trying to protect my people if war were ever to happen. We are a peaceful kingdom here in Mormhuir Cathair." Cullen wasn't sure he would be able to help. The journey here took them over three days across the very harsh terrain. If Luke ever needed his help, it would be a long trip for his army. However, the added benefit of a seaport trade sounded good.

"Luke, you have lived in peace for so many years. Why now, are you suddenly concerned that war may come?"

Luke looked nervous. "Haven't you heard the legend?"

Cullen tried not to look surprised. *Is he talking about the legend of my people?* He thought.

Luke continued, "I have heard of a kingdom that is very strong now, but one day, they would conquer all their enemies. No one would be able to conquer them."

Cullen sat a little straighter in his seat as he noticed the shocked expression on Marcus' face. "Yes, I have heard of that legend," Cullen said, "Why would that legend scare you? If you are a peaceful country, it sounds like you have no need to worry. The legend does say they would conquer all their enemies, right?"

Luke seemed confused, "Yes, that is what the legend says."

"Well then," Cullen continued, "If you are not their enemy, you have nothing to worry about." Cullen turned to Marcus, "Wouldn't you agree, Marcus?"

"Yes, my lord."

Luke turned toward Cullen. "So, does that mean you will not join with me as my ally?"

"No, all that means is I don't think you should be worried about getting an ally. However, if you think you need our help that badly, we will come to your aid. Keep in mind that we are several days journey away. I don't think we would be much help if you were attacked by sea. By the time your messenger got to us, and we assembled and came to your aid, over a week would have passed."

"Perhaps you are right," Luke said. "I do try to keep peace with all my neighboring kingdoms, but I think just knowing that you are one of my allies, I would sleep better at night."

"Very well, friends we will be. I look forward to trading with you, although that mountain pass will make that quite difficult." Cullen said with a smile. "Consider us your allies."

Luke chuckled. "You're right, it is quite silly of me to ask for your help, but still, I am grateful for your willingness to come to my aide."

After the meeting with King Luke. Cullen and Marcus decided to look around the seaport village.

"Marcus, go to the marketplace and purchase the items we may need for our return trip home. Also, look for something special for your wife and the baby. Consider it a gift from me. No price is too great. I want to look around this village."

"Yes, my lord. Thank you," Marcus replied as he turned and headed to the marketplace.

As Cullen walked the streets, he remembered the woman that he used to hear. *I wonder whatever happened to her,* he thought. As he walked by the fishing boats, he stopped to watch the fishermen unload their catch of the day.

In the distance, he saw a strikingly beautiful woman. She had long wavy blonde hair that shimmered in the sunlight. A large man stood arguing with her about the price of the fish she wanted to buy. Cullen approached just in case this man would cause problems. Watching from a distance, Cullen felt as if he had seen her before, many years ago. *Why does she look so familiar?* He wondered as he watched the conversation. She boldly challenged the fisherman.

"I said that fish is worth this basket of vegetables and no more! If you don't want these vegetables, I don't want your fish."

The fisherman looked at the ground as he shuffled his feet in the dirt. "Fine, I will only trade with you because my wife needs those vegetables. Now, get a real job woman, because haggling in the market is not good. People could take advantage of a woman alone in the marketplace," he said as he turned to leave.

Wow, Keela thought to herself, *haggling for food is difficult. Why can't I find a regular job?*

"Excuse me."

Startled, Keela turned around to see a man standing a short distance away. When she turned, Cullen could see the beauty of her face. She had brown eyes, and they were bright and alive.

"I'm sorry, I didn't mean to startle you." He said.

"How long have you been standing there?"

"Oh, just a few minutes. I waited until you were finished speaking with the fisherman."

Standing next to him caused her to stand straighter to look directly into his face. She determined that he stood several inches taller than her. He had to be about five feet, nine inches, quite a bit taller and most men in the village. She looked directly into his face. His expression was kind and gentle, while his bright blue eyes were almost piercing. It seemed like light radiated from them. He had dark brown hair trimmed to his shoulders. He did not dress like an ordinary villager, and she couldn't remember seeing him in town before.

"I don't think I have seen you in the village before."

"No, you wouldn't have seen me, I am just passing through. I have been traveling for quite some time. Could I buy some of those vegetables from you? I haven't enjoyed any fresh vegetable since my journey began and I know my horse would enjoy a few carrots also."

"Of course, you may purchase my vegetables. However, I only have a few with me here. I have more in the field over there, please come with me."

As they walked toward the field, Keela wondered about this man, *Should I even be walking out of the safety of the village to give him more carrots? What if he was the type of person the fisherman talked about?* She shivered at the thought. She needed money, and she needed to take this risk. She didn't have a home any longer because she hadn't found a job soon enough. The king's friends were gracious to keep her as long as they did. Although now she had no home, she was grateful for the King's gift. The king had given her a small piece of land to grow her vegetables for trade so that she wouldn't starve. Now she needed to save enough money to find shelter before winter came.

As Cullen filled his bags with vegetables and fed a few carrots to Hunter. Keela studied him. *He seems like a kind person,* she thought. His expression did not hold anything that gave her fear. She felt protected around him. *I wonder where he's traveling from, and where he is going? Should I ask if I could go with him? No! That's a ridiculous thought. If only I knew him better, then I would ask.*

Cullen turned away from his bags and handed Keela a small leather pouch filled with coins, "Here, this should pay for the vegetables."

When she took the bag from him, her arm sank slightly from its weight. "Oh, no. This is way too much money, I would never ask for so much!"

Cullen laughed a lighthearted laugh, "You don't even know how much I gave you. Perhaps it's filled with stone!"

"I guess you're right, but somehow, you don't seem to be that kind of person. You seem very trustworthy."

"Trustworthy?! What have I done to earn any trust? I have a feeling you're the kind of person who believes in people until they prove they are not worth trusting."

Keela felt the heat rise in her face; she felt like she had been punched. "Is there something wrong with believing in people?" She said.

"No, nothing wrong with it, you just need to be careful, many people are not worth trusting. They might take advantage of someone like you."

Hadn't she heard that already once today? "Well, thank you. I'll think about what you said."

Still trying to remember why he felt like knew her, he said. "May I ask, what is your name?"

Keela suddenly felt shy. "My friends call me Keela," she said.

Cullen thought to himself. *Well, I don't know of anyone called Keela, it must be my imagination. Maybe I remember someone who reminds me of her.* "Keela," Cullen said the name slowly, "That's a beautiful name, and it suits you well."

Keela wasn't sure what he meant by that. "Why do you say that my name suits me?"

Cullen turned and looked her directly in the eyes. "Because Keela means Beautiful."

Keela felt like her heart skip a beat or two. *What am I supposed to say to that?* She thought. Keela could feel the heat rise in her face as she turned away. "Thank you," She mumbled quietly.

"You don't believe me, do you?"

Cullen's question had taken her by surprise. "I'm just not used to compliments," Keela stammered.

Sensing her awkwardness, Cullen looked around. "Why are you selling your vegetables way over here? You're not near your house, and you're not near the village market. I don't understand."

How could she make him leave? He began to make her uncomfortable. Keela looked down. "This is my house, sir," she whispered.

Cullen could not believe what she just said! Did she just imply that she had no home? "You mean to tell me that you don't have a home?! A woman like you should be in a house safe and protected by her husband. Are you married? Where is your husband? Where are your parents?" The astonishment still on his face as he stared into her brown eyes.

"I don't know who my parents are. I am an orphan, raised by a group of nuns. Once I reached a certain age, they set me off to make my way in the world. I'll be fine, don't worry. I just need to find work, then get a place to call home."

Cullen looked at her with new eyes. No wonder she had been so bold with the fisherman; she needed food. She needed to haggle in the marketplace to survive. He wanted to help her find a place to stay. "Keela, let me help you."

She turned to him challenging him with her eyes alone, ready for a fight. "I don't need handouts. I will be fine on my own," she said with determination.

Cullen knew he would not be able to change her mind, and he didn't want to argue about it. Silently, Cullen returned to his saddlebag and retrieved another larger leather bag.

"Sorry to hear that you're struggling to make it. That small bag of money won't go too far. Please take this; it will help you get on your feet," Cullen said as he held the pouch toward Keela.

"I don't want your sympathy. I'll be fine!" She pushed the leather pouch away refusing his gift. Even though defiance filled her voice, her voice wavered showing that tears were threatening to fall. Cullen knew he had upset her.

"I know you will be fine. You are a strong woman with good character. Forgive me for upsetting you. I wish you would reconsider taking my gift."

Keela held her chin high. "I don't want handouts." She said as she turned slightly away from Cullen.

Cullen let out a deep sigh. "Well, I must continue on my journey then. I need to meet up with my friend, and we will continue our trip. I pray that you will receive a bountiful harvest, a warm home, and health to your bones." Keela had not turned toward him or even acknowledge his comments, so he quietly walked back to Hunter.

Keela still had questions. In the corner of her eye, she saw him walk away. Turning towards him, she almost called him back to keep talking but decided it would be better if she left it alone. This strange traveler impacted her. She would remember him for a long time. Sadness filled her heart as she watched him mount his horse, with a nod of his head he turned his horse around and left without saying another word.

Legend

On the journey home from Mormhuir Cathair, Cullen decided now would be an excellent time to travel to Nochtadh to research the legend.

"Marcus, go ahead home and take care of Moria, I am going to the ancient library."

"More questions, my lord?"

"Yes, my mind is full of questions. I thought if I can reread the parchment, maybe I will find some answers."

"Very well, my lord."

Marcus headed south towards home, as Cullen turned Hunter towards Nochtadh.

Nochtadh, once a busy village had become a very sleepy town. Years ago, people felt it was too far from Dia Richoet and vulnerable to attack. Many of the cottages had been left empty by their owners, thick vines chocked and covered the abandoned homes. Cullen led Hunter through the main street until he came to the library. The library remained clean and well-kept despite the wild undergrowth that grew a short distance from the door. Slowly, Cullen entered the library. Once his eyes adjusted to the dimly lit room, he saw the sage sitting at a desk near the window.

"Good day, Conary!"

The old gentleman looked up from his book. "King Cullen? What do I have the pleasure of your company for?" Conary said with a stunned look on his face.

"Conary, I want to read the parchment that explains the legend."

The expression on Conary's face changed from surprise to joy. "My lord, I would be happy to get that for you. It's one of my favorite reads."

Just a short time later, Conary handed Cullen an ancient parchment. "Forgive me for asking, my lord, but is there something specific you are looking for?"

"I just wanted to study it again, It has been years…" Cullen said as he opened the scroll to begin to read. Slowly, he sat in the chair next to the window as he continued to read.

Most of the Legend had been what he remembered; the story of a limitless kingdom. A king and queen who could speak to each other through their thoughts. A territory that remained in peace for many generations because of the boundless love the king and queen shared. However, there were parts of the legend that he had forgotten. According to the legend, the woman who would later become the queen was held in captivity and tormented by her foes.

Cullen's mind raced. *Am I the king in the legend? What is this woman's name?* Cullen wished the legend gave the names of the king and queen. *Perhaps the woman is receiving a severe beating even now.* Cullen thought back to the times he had spoken with her in his dreams. Their conversations were brief. Cullen remembered one thing she said, someone named King Luke was holding her. Cullen only knew one Luke. He had just met with King Luke. They discussed the legend and how he wanted to have Cullen as an ally. Cullen shook his head, *No, it can't be King Luke. He wouldn't throw an innocent woman in the dungeon.* Instantly Cullen remembered the woman selling her vegetables to the fisherman. Closing his eyes, he could still envision her face. *Why did she look so familiar to me?* Just then a thought occurred to him.

"Conary!"

"Yes, my lord,"

"Do you have any paintings of any kind of King Oscar and his wife, Aideen?"

"Yes, my lord, we have their family painting, where Aideen is holding her daughter. Probably about one year before they were killed."

"Excellent. I would like to see it."

Just a few moments later, Conary handed him the painting. Cullen's hand trembled slightly. The woman in the marketplace looked just like Queen Aideen. *Why didn't I see the resemblance before?* Picking up the ancient parchment, he re-read the story again. If she was brutally beaten, how can he help his betrothed? Soon he found his answer. If the king laid down his life freely to pay for her freedom, as an act of pure, selfless love, the woman would be allowed to go free and love its self would give life back to the king. This would prove that love is stronger than death. *If that was Sine, she was not locked in a dungeon. It must be talking about someone else.* Cullen carefully wrapped the scroll and handed it back to Conary.

"My lord, are you alright?"

Cullen gave him a weak smile, "I'm fine Conary, I just need some fresh air. Thank you for getting this parchment for me. I need to get going now."

"Good day, sir," Conary shouted as Cullen left the library, closing the door behind him.

Lurking Danger

Marcus needed to patrol one of the southern villages. Many villagers were trying to complete the bountiful harvest before the first snow fell. He watched as entire families worked side by side in the fields. Each field he came to appeared to be the same; families working hard together, even young children. In one area, Marcus noticed one young boy at the far end of the field. The boy was with a man, and the two of them were talking. *That must be his father,* Marcus thought, *Strange that they are so far away from where everyone else is working.* Marcus turned and looked at the families near him. They had now harvested most of the field.

"Good day, sir," Marcus said to the farmer closest to him. The man looked up and nodded.

"Good day."

"Looks as if you should have no trouble harvesting your field before the snow comes."

The man looked up from his labor again, "Yes, sir. The weather has been holding out, and the good Lord has given us the strength to reap the bountiful harvest he provided for us. If we work hard, we might be able to finish the work before nightfall. These old bones of mine are telling me, that snow will fall tonight."

Marcus thought back to the man and his son far across the field. "Excuse me, but can I ask if you are almost finished, why are people still working on the far side of the field?"

The man looked at Marcus, "There is nothing on the far side of the field. Did you see people working them?"

"Yes, a man and a young boy. Being at a distance, I couldn't see…" Marcus stopped talking as he noticed the expression on the man's face had changed. He looked around him nervously. "Is everything alright?"

"Sorry," the man said, "You mentioned a young boy, and I realized that I had not seen my son recently. He tends to wander off when he should be working. Peter!" he yelled, "Peter, where are you?!" The man turned toward another young man working by his side." Have you seen Peter?"

"Dad, you know he always disappears when it's time to work. I'm sure he will come home after we have finished."

The man did not seem happy with the boy's answer. Turning to Marcus, he said. "Please sir, could you help me find my son? Where did you see the man and the boy?"

"They were in this field," he said as he pointed to the field behind him. "They were in the far corner almost into the woods. I will go that way and see if I can locate them."

"His name is Peter. Thank you for your help. I will search closer to the barn and house here just in case he is hiding from work."

Marcus headed out across the field. He did not see the man or the boy anymore. *They couldn't have gotten too far,* Marcus thought. As he neared the edge of the woods, he could hear voices.

"Come on boy; I have the perfect place for you. You will never have to work for your father again."

"I-I-I don't know." the child responded, "I don't think I should go with you. My dad will be looking for me."

The pitch in the man's voice changed quickly. He began speaking to the boy in a low, gruff voice which almost sounded like a growl. "You're coming with me kid! That's it! Your dad can't help you now; you're too far away he can't hear you!"

Fear became evident in the child's voice. "No! I said I didn't want to go with you!" He said as his voice wavered with emotion.

The bushes had given Marcus just the cover he needed to remain hidden as he listened to the conversation. Now he could no longer stay silent.

Marcus stepped out from behind the bushes that were between himself and the young boy.

"Peter, it's alright. This man's not going to take you anywhere." Marcus said as he stepped in front of Peter. He used his arms to shelter Peter and keep him behind his back. "Peter, go home." Turning toward the man, he said, "You heard the boy, he doesn't want to go with you."

The man that stood before Marcus was furious at this point. His green eyes were beady and filled with rage as he shouted at Marcus.

"Get out of my way. This does not concern you in any way."

"It concerns me completely. I will not allow you to force this child to go with you."

Marcus had already taken into consideration the size of this man. Size did not intimidate him. He had learned years ago that sometimes being smaller can be a significant advantage. Marcus noticed that the armor the man wore bore the emblem of Chrioch Olc. No doubt he would fight like a warrior.

"Well, we shall see about that," the attacker snarled. Without warning, the man punched Marcus directly in the face. Determined to win this fight, Marcus gave several punches to the man's face. Marcus knew this would be a difficult fight. Looking for an advantage, he saw thorny thicket behind the man. Marcus Lunged at the man, forcing him to step back briefly losing his balance. As the spikes cut deep into the backs of the man's legs, he pulled a knife from his belt and lunged toward Marcus. Marcus stumbled on the branches at his feet, falling to the ground. Immediately, he reached for a sturdy branch. In one swift movement, he blocked the man's attack with the knife, only inches from his face.

The man's crushing weight held Marcus securely to the ground. His arms trembled as he used all his strength just to keep the knife from slashing his throat.

"Ha, now I got you. You think you're a better fighter than me?

You are nothing! I will kill you for trying to interfere," The attacker growled as he gave a cruel laugh.

The struggle continued for a few moments. Marcus began to wonder if this would be his final battle. Suddenly, he heard a sickening crack sound. The attacker fell limp on top of Marcus.

Pushing the man off him, Marcus quickly jumped to his feet, taking the knife from the attacker's motionless hand. Marcus saw Peter standing in front of him. The boy stood trembling head to foot, all color had drained from his face. In his right hand, he held a sturdy club. Turning his attention to the boy, Marcus said,

"Why are you still here? I told you to go home."

As tears filled the boy's eyes, he could only nod his head. "Are you okay?" The boy whispered, "You're hurt." Peter stammered.

Marcus could feel the pulsating pain that was emanating from his lip. "I'm fine, really." Marcus felt guilty for scolding the boy who quite possibly just saved his life. "That was a very courageous thing you did."

"Why did you do that? He could have killed you," Peter said, his voice still trembling.

"I did it to protect you. Although, you're the one who quite possibly just saved my life. I'm sorry I scolded you. Thank you for your help. However, you should have run as fast as you could back to your father's house. What if I lost that fight? That horrible man would have taken you."

"Why? I mean why did you protect me?" Peter asked.

"You needed protection, didn't you? Besides it's my job." Not wanting the boy to ask any more questions Marcus continued, "Ready to go back home? Your father is looking for you."

Winter Coming

Cullen couldn't stop thinking about the beautiful young lady he had met in Mormhuir Cathair. Her face haunted his mind. *Why do I feel like I knew her? She seems so familiar.* He thought back to that day. Her attitude remained upbeat and cheerful even though she had no place to call home. It was apparent that she was a beautiful woman who was not afraid to be herself. Apparently, she hadn't been homeless for long, her clothes and appearance were still very fresh. *Why was she homeless? Did she have a husband?* When he asked her about her husband, she didn't answer. She merely spoke about her upbringing. The thought bothered Cullen that perhaps someone in his kingdom struggled the same way. He called in his guard, Quinn.

"Yes, my lord?"

Quinn, a wise older gentleman, determined that despite his age would serve as a guard. Cullen kept him as a guard in the castle, not because of his age, but because of his wisdom.

"I need a census of all the people in each village in my kingdom. I want to know if every person has a place to call home. I don't want a single person to be without a roof over their head this winter. Report back to me as soon as the results have come in from every village."

"My lord, that's a huge task so close to winter. May I ask why you are concerned about that now?"

"Quinn, I don't feel I need to explain myself. Please, just report back to me when you have completed the census," Cullen said gently.

"Yes, sir," Quinn said as he turned to leave the room.

Cullen thought, *that will soothe my mind for a little while. If only that woman lived in my kingdom, then her needs would be met.* Surprised by his desire to protect this woman he had barely met.

Keela's clothing had become threadbare and tattered from working the land and carrying her basket to the market each day. A kind elderly woman had given her a cloak when fall began, but even that had become torn by the thicket that surrounded the place she called home. She wrapped the tattered cloak closer. Discouragement settled in her heart as the cold, damp evening air penetrated her bones. *How am I going to survive the winter outside? Well, the sisters were wrong. They thought I was ready to live on my own. Ready to start my own life. What would they think of me now? Perhaps I could go back to them and beg them to let me stay at least through the winter. They wouldn't turn me away, would they?* Keela thought about the sisters she had loved. Many of them were like her best friends, but she knew Mother Sara. If the rules of the convent said Keela would not be allowed back into the convent, she would say no.

As a storm gathered on the horizon, Keela tried to find anything that she could consider a shelter. She needed to find a way out of the rain or snow and found an area on the outskirts of the field where a fallen pine tree created a small shelter. She looked under the pine branches. *Well,* she thought, *it's small, but hopefully, it will protect me from the storm a little.* The evergreen branches were still full and green. That would help keep the snow off her. As Keela climbed under the fallen tree, she heard her skirt tear as it got caught on a branch. *Great, I don't need any more rips in this!* She barely had enough room to pull her legs close to her chest as she tried to keep herself warm. Slowly, she drifted off into a light sleep.

Keela awoke surprised to find that she slept under a blanket of snow. Her legs shivered so uncontrollably; she didn't know if she could stand without her knees knocking together. *How am I going to survive this winter?!* Fear started to take hold of her heart. Angrily, she swiped at the tears that found their way down her cheeks. *No time to feel sorry for myself, I need to find a home.*

Keela stood and shook the snow from her clothes. Determination settled in her heart. She decided to take control of the situation instead of letting fear take control of her. *Okay,* she thought, *I have searched for a place to live and a job here, maybe I should try a different village. I might have a better chance at finding a place to stay, or perhaps someone would have pity on me and take me in.* The field that the king allowed her to use had been nice, but she could not stay there through the winter. Keela headed east away from Mormhuir Cathair. Wherever this road would lead, she would make the best of it.

Ronan

Cullen stood looking out his window. He loved the freshly fallen snow. It always reminded him of a new beginning, a fresh start. Before he could enjoy its beauty, he needed to know that everyone in his villages had a place to call home.

"Quinn!"

Immediately the older gentleman stepped into the room. "Yes, my lord."

"Since I asked for a census of all the people who had no home, how many have we found homes for?"

"My lord, it has been difficult, but we have been able to find a house for every person that did not have a home."

"Everyone? Are you sure?"

"I believe so, my lord. Your craftsmen have been very busy building shelters for families and the few that we had not prepared a home for are either living with other families temporarily or are living in the servants' quarters of the castle until a home is made available for them."

"Thank You, Quinn. I think I will walk through the villages to make sure no one is left outside in this cold. Care to come with me?"

"Yes, sir."

As Cullen and Quinn walked through the streets of the local village, Cullen didn't notice a single beggar left on the streets. They continued their journey on horseback as they went from village to village.

"My Lord, it is getting dark. Shouldn't we head back?"

"Quinn, my friend, you have done your job well. I have not found anyone without a home, but I cannot sleep well tonight until I am sure we have searched every community. This is the last village; soon we will head home."

Cullen was content knowing that every beggar was safe and warm for the winter. Now he would work on how to help them further. As Quinn and Cullen turned their horses and headed back toward the castle, Cullen chose a road that would be a more direct route home. The trail went directly across the farmer's fields and pastures. After traveling for a short distance, Hunter stopped short.

"What is it, boy?" Cullen tried to urge Hunter forward, "Walk!" Leaning forward in his saddle, Cullen saw what got Hunter's attention. There, on the side of the road, a man lay in the frost covered grass. Immediately both Quinn and Cullen dismounted their horses. The man appeared to be half frozen. Quinn leaned his ear close to the man's face and listened for a breath.

"He's alive, my lord," Quinn said Quietly. "Not sure if he will survive though."

"Let's take him to the village doctor."

Cullen and Quinn carefully wrapped the man in the blankets they had attached to the saddles. When Cullen picked up the man, his heart ached. His weight was very light for a grown man.

"He must be starved! He's as heavy as a young child. Quinn, walk Hunter. The village is not far, I will carry this man to the local doctor and see if we can save him."

A short time later, Quinn and Cullen left the man in the care of a local doctor and his family.

"Thank you for nursing this man back to health. Any costs that you incur I will repay, all you need to do is ask."

Once Cullen knew the doctor would do anything he could to save the man, they headed home. Now, their only light was given to them by the bright full moon. The bitter winds blew across the fields. Quinn and Cullen wrapped their cloaks tightly around themselves and tried their best to hide their faces from the stinging cold. *I wouldn't want to live out here in this cold,* Cullen thought to himself. Again, he found himself wondering about Keela, *I hope she found a warm shelter. Oh, if only she lived in my kingdom then I would know for sure her needs would be met.*

"My lord," Quinn said "If it pleases you since it is late in the evening, allow me to go directly to my house. My wife must have dinner waiting."

"Of course," Cullen replied. He brought Hunter to a stop. "Quinn, I know I thanked you earlier for your hard work. But, seeing a man like that, who we quite possibly saved from death tonight, makes me grateful to have excellent men like yourself serving me. Thanks again"

Quinn looked slightly embarrassed. "My lord, you do not need to thank me. I am grateful to serve you as King."

"Now, go home to your wife, warm your bones and rest well."

"Yes, Sir."

As Cullen entered the courtyard, a stable hand came to meet him. "Good evening, my lord, I trust you had a safe ride?"

"Yes, but it sure is cold out there," Cullen replied. "Please take good care of Hunter. Make sure he is warm and well fed."

"Yes, my lord."

Cullen dismounted and left Hunter in the capable hands of the stable worker. Cullen walked into the warmth of the castle and immediately heard the commotion going on in the open courtroom. Voices were getting loud and urgent. Cullen walked into the courtroom to find out what caused the disturbance. Before he entered the room, he heard,

"Help! I need someone to help my wife!"

Instantly Cullen recognized the voice. "Marcus! What's going on? Is the baby coming?"

"Yes, and I can't find Nancy or the doctor!"

Immediately, Cullen called for his head maidservants and told them to go to Marcus' house as fast as possible. Marcus and Cullen headed for the horse stables to get the horses ready for the maids to ride.

Moria didn't want to admit it to Marcus, but everything about this baby seemed wrong. Now, with all the pain, she tried to stand up, but she wasn't strong enough. The pain would have her on the floor in no time. In her desperation, she thought, *where did Marcus go? Why would he leave me now? Nancy promised she would be right here for her; she only lived next door. How long did it take to walk next door?* Moria heard voices at the door, and two women that Moria never saw before walked in. Moria looked confused, soon another bout of pain washed over her. She had no chance to ask questions. Immediately both women were at her side. The older one explained that they were the head maids from the castle and Cullen has told them to come because Marcus could not find the doctor or Nancy.

"I feel like I have to stand up! I am so exhausted … please, help me, I don't know what to do!" Moria exclaimed between breaths.

The two women exchanged glances, expressions of fear evident on their faces. "We are not strong enough to help you stand. Remain here on the bed for now, when the pain comes again, tell us if you feel like you are ready to push," The older woman said.

A few more waves of pain crashed over her. She felt like this nightmare would never end. Just then, the door burst open, and a very ashen faced Marcus came bolting through the door, breathless from running.

"I started to think you left me," Moria moaned.

"Honey, I would never leave you. Not now. Not ever."

"Please, help me stand. I have this incredible urge to stand, but I'm too tired."

Marcus was relieved as he watched Nancy walk into the room just as Moria said those words.

"Should I help her stand?" he asked.

"Of course, you should help her. I haven't seen that happen very often, but the times I have, the child came quickly."

It took all the strength that Marcus could muster to lift his wife and hold her back against himself. As the pain would crash over Moria, Marcus tried to say things into her ear to encourage her. Although he wasn't sure she heard a word, every time she cried out, she seemed to get heavier. Marcus realized that although he held her up, she kept trying to stand on her own, but when the pain came, she had no strength at all.

"Almost there!" he heard Nancy say, "Just a few more seconds and all this will be behind you. Just think of how it will feel to be holding your precious child in your arms."

As the next wave of pain came, Moria let out such a cry, Marcus felt as if someone ripped his heart out, He refused to let fear take hold of his mind. *I have to be strong for Moria,* he thought. After another cry, he began praying, *Oh, God, don't let her die! Please! I can't lose Moria.* A tear slowly slid down his cheek at the thought of losing her. Just then, her cry turned into a type of cry/laugh.

"It's over! right?" Moria's voice sounded very hoarse. Marcus, so relieved to hear it, he almost broke down and cried. He didn't know what made him happier, hearing that he had a healthy baby boy or just the sound of Moria voice.

"Yes, you have given birth to a beautiful, strong baby boy."

Marcus gently lowered Moria back onto the bed. Nancy and the other maids continued to work around Moria, but neither Marcus nor Moria seemed to notice anything but the face of their baby boy.

Cullen rejoiced with Moria and Marcus for their new baby boy. They named him Ronan. Someday, Cullen would have a family. He remembered that his father had arranged to be married to Sine, a princess from the kingdom of Esperanza. Unfortunately, the domain became unsettled; war broke out after the king and queen had been killed. No one knew what had happened to Sine. Cullen wondered if he should try to find her. Weren't his marriage arrangements still intact?

Captured

Keela decided to head south. As she walked, she shivered so severely, her teeth chattered uncontrollably, and her stomach grumbled in protest to the small amount of food she had given it. She felt the fear rush into her heart. She didn't know what she feared most, dying in the cold, or walking into the woods again. *What is it about the forest that scares me so much?* She wondered *I should just lie down in the snow and die. I'm sure the cold would numb my senses, and I would just fall asleep,* she thought.

Suddenly, a large, dirty hand reached from behind her head and covered her mouth. She tried to get loose and fight, but his strength overwhelmed her no matter what she did. She tried to run, but He grabbed her arm and spun her around to face him. His eyes were green, and they seemed to be filled with anger and bitterness.

"You're coming with me," He hissed through clenched teeth. "If you don't come willingly, I will force you to come, I have my ways, and let me tell you, they are not pleasant."

The fear in Keela's heart seemed to fill every part of her being. She had never been treated so harshly, and she didn't know what she had ever done. This man looked sick. His skin had an ashen colored appearance and his black hair matted to his head. She saw noticeable bruises on his face. *Did he get into a fight recently?* She wondered.

Too afraid to argue with the man, Keela stood slowly, trying to steady herself. Her head began pounding so hard now; she felt dizzy.

The last thing she wanted to do was stumble in the snow. She had a feeling that this man would have no sympathy for her. Roughly, he pulled her to his side. He gripped her arm so hard she winced in pain.

"Walk!" He spat out the word through clenched teeth.

Keela began to move forward. Hidden in the bushes, Keela saw a horse laden down with animal furs and other burdens. The man walked to the horse and removed a rope that had been hanging over the horse's saddle. He turned and roughly tied her hands together and fastened the other end to the horse's saddle after he mounted the horse. She tried to walk with the most dignity that she could muster, but that soon diminished.

The bitter cold wind felt like a knife to her exposed skin. *When are we going to stop rest?! If I fall in this snow, I'm sure he will just drag me along. God, if you're out there, help me, please!* Almost as soon as Keela prayed that prayer, the man on the horse stopped short. He turned and looked at her and gruffly said,

"We will stay here for the night."

As the sun began to set, Keela determined that they were heading south.

"Please tell me where we are going."

The man sat facing the fire with his back toward Keela. He never said a word. Sitting just outside of the reach of the fire's heat, Keela shivered. *What did I ever do? He's acting as if I am not even here. I wish I knew where we are going or what he wants with me.* Keela's feet were hurting her badly. She carefully removed her shoes and saw that blisters had begun to form and several of them were bleeding. She winced as she put the cold snow on her feet. *Maybe that will keep them from swelling too much and stop the bleeding. How long is he going to make me walk,* she wondered.

The man got up, went to his horse, and removed his bedding material. In her view, he set up his bedding nice and close to the fire. Then he turned towards Keela, licking his lips he chuckled.

"Do you want to sleep with me by the fire?" he said with a mocking smile. The expression on his face made Keela shiver "I will keep you warm for the night." Again, he chuckled.

Keela did not say a word. After a few moments of silence, she watched his expression turn angry. He stormed over to her and tightened the knots in the rope that tied her securely to a tree

"Then stay over here and freeze!" he thundered as he turned back and headed to the fire.

Keela didn't sleep at all that night. She felt chilled to the bone. Keela sat with her knees tucked as close to her chest as possible. Her teeth chattered together, and her fingers were numb. As dawn broke, Keela allowed her thoughts to return to the time she spent in Mormhuir Cathair. *Things were not this bad in that village. Why didn't I just stay there, eventually I would have found a place to stay, right?* The face of the traveler came to her memory. *Didn't he try to warn me? I wonder whatever happened to him.* She noticed the man began to stir from his bed. She watched as he got up, rolled up his bedding and fastened it to the horse. Silently, he turned and came toward Keela. Untying her feet, he shouted, "Walk!"

As dawn broke and the sun began to make its way across the landscape, Keela noticed the steep mountain terrain changed into rolling hills. Stone walls seemed to appear everywhere she looked. Many times, they needed to change course to go around the stone walls. Twice the man untied her and allowed his horse to jump over the stone walls. Keela struggled over the walls with her hands still fastened by the rope. She walked all through the day until she sure she would fall.

Unexpectedly, the man stopped and dismounted the horse. Without a word, he tied her feet together, picked her up and tossed her on the back of the horse. She heard a crack sound as she landed on the horse. The pain was so excruciating; she could not help but cry out in pain. Her ribs hurt, her feet were throbbing in pain and now, watching the ground move by the horses' feet, Keela felt very sick. After a short time, they stopped.

"Ok, enough of a free ride, get off! It's your turn to walk."

He pulled her off the back of the horse, cut the ropes off her feet and put her on the ground, she stumbled and fell into a pile in the snow.

"I can't walk."

"Well, then I'll just drag you. I would rather walk if I were you."

As Keela struggled to her feet, she felt extremely weak. The excruciating pain made her wonder how long she would be able to walk. Keela saw a dense forest directly in front of them. *Why do we have to go into the forest? Keela thought as fear gripped her heart again. Isn't it bad enough that I'm captured and forced to walk? I feel like my ribs are broken, and my head is pounding. God, if you're out there help me, please!*

As night fell, the man stopped and made a fire. Just like before, he slept next to the fire and left her tied to a tree just outside the warmth of the fire. Even though the cold, bitter, wind made strange sounds as it howled in the branches, Keela fell into a profound sleep. As she slept, she dreamed. The dream was not a fearful dream, but very peaceful. She felt as if she slept in a warm bed. Someone spoke to her in the dream, although she could not remember any of the words, peace filled her senses. Suddenly, Keela was awakened by a firm shake of her shoulder.

"Get up woman! It's time to walk."

As Keela looked around, she noticed something in the light of day that she did not see last night, a castle in the distance.

Cullen woke with a start. His heart pounded so hard he thought it could be heard in the next room. He wiped the bead of perspiration from his forehead. *Why am I dreaming like that again? Why did it feel so real!* Cullen felt his heartbeat slow down to the regular pattern. He got out of bed and went to look out his window. As he stood looking out the window, he tried to remember anything he could about the dream. One thing that remained very clear, it was cold, so cold his hands still ached. He remembered the feeling of the ropes digging into his wrists and the pulsating pain in his feet. The dream ended abruptly Cullen heard a man's voice yelling, Cullen knew that voice anywhere, it was Philip, the captain of King Dorcha's army. *If she is held by King Dorcha, I will need to find a way to get into the dungeon without being noticed,* Cullen thought, *Perhaps Kelly could give me some advice.* After breakfast, Cullen summoned Kelly to come and speak with him. Kelly entered the room looking a little apprehensive,

"My lord, you summoned me?"

"Yes, Kelly, I need to ask you about King Dorcha's army and castle."

Kelly looked surprised. "My lord? You plan on going to Dorcha's domain?"

"Kelly, I can't get into all the details right now, but someone is being held in Dorcha's dungeon, and I am going to get them out."

Kelly was silent for a few minutes. "My lord, that is very perilous, and it may cost you your life. I wish you would reconsider. Perhaps send someone else in your place. I will go for you, just give the word."

"Kelly, Thank you for your loyalty and concern. I understand your caution, just know that I am fully aware of how dangerous this is. That will not change my mind. This is something I need to do."

Kelly hesitated to object again," I am not to tell you what to do. If you still want to go, be careful. When you enter the courtyard, seek out my brother Aaron."

"Can Aaron be trusted?"

"I trust Aaron with my life. He is the one who assisted me when my family and I fled the empire. Aaron will help you appear as one of Dorcha's soldiers and get you into the dungeon. Tell him I sent you but don't tell him who you are."

Dungeon

Despite the objection from his best friend, the captain of his army, Cullen knew he needed to head south. As he saddled and mounted Hunter, he thought back to last night when he heard her again. He could envision the dungeon cell where she sat. The bed in her dungeon cell stood just outside of her reach because the chains were too short, she could not reach the bed. He refused to give up until he found her and rescued her.

King Dorcha had no mercy toward any person. Several of his own men had requested safe haven in Dia Richoet. Cullen thought back to the day Kelly, now one of his most trusted men, came to him asking for help. Marcus found one of Dorcha's soldier traveling into the village near the castle. Thinking that he was spying, Marcus brought him before King Cullen. There, on his knees before Cullen, he made his request known.

"My lord," he cried, "Please have mercy on my family. I am seeking refuge from King Dorcha. If he knows I came to you for help, I will surely die. My wife and son would also be killed."

Cullen did not say a word for a moment. The young man before him began to look around anxiously.

"What is your name?" Cullen asked.

"Kelly, my lord."

"Why am I to believe that you and your family only want to seek refuge? How do you defend yourself with the accusation that you are a spy?"

The young man stood and looked Cullen directly in the eye.

"My lord, I can only give you my word that I am not a spy. However, if it pleases you, take my life. I only ask that you spare my family."

Cullen admired the young man's courage and determination to keep his family safe. Cullen noticed a young woman standing off to the side of the room. Tears are streaming down her face as she cradled a newborn in her arms. Cullen could tell by the dusty attire, that they had just traveled a great distance. Turning toward the woman, he said," Come here."

Nervously she came toward Cullen.

"Let me hold the child."

She looked stunned, and the color quickly drained from her face. Nervously, she turned to look at Kelly. Kelly gave a slight nod to her, and with trembling hands, she gave her newborn son to Cullen then turned to stand by Kelly's side. Cullen could still remember the dirty, tear-stained face of that little boy. His heart ached to think of how terrible the journey must have been for both the boy and his mother.

Turning his attention back to Kelly he said, "I will grant you and your young family safe haven within my kingdom. I do not believe you would have made a very young child and his mother travel such a distance just to spy on me."

At once the young woman let out a cry of relief and clung to Kelly as she began to sob. "Thank you, my lord,"

She said between sobs. Kelly looked like a statue, just standing strong with this eye unmoving from Cullen's face.

"My lord, you have shown us great mercy. I pledge my life to you."

Cullen rose from his throne and walked a few feet to where the couple stood.

"Here is your son."

Kelly took his son from him and bowed low before Cullen. "Thank you again, my lord; you will not regret the mercy you have shown to my family and me."

Cullen shook his head to clear the memory. The stories that Kelly told about King Dorcha were enough to make Cullen's skin crawl. Cullen knew if Dorcha had the woman locked in the dungeon, it would be no easy task to get her free. Determined, he turned Hunter to the south.

Keela had not seen daylight for many weeks now. Staying in the cold darkness, it felt as if a dense fog had clouded her thinking; she had completely lost track of time. Her body was sore all over and the wounds on her back from yesterday's whipping, had not yet begun to heal. She tried to move to get a little comfort. Short shackles were attached to the wall had been placed on her ankles. The chains allowed for a bit of movement, but they did not allow her to reach her bed. Her tongue was swollen, and her head pounded from lack of water. The little bit of moldy bread and rotten vegetable that was given to her as a meal were thrown on the floor. Even if she could reach it, the rats would get it first. It was a miracle that she slept at all during the night.

However, she didn't just sleep; she slept peacefully. Again, last night, she had that same lingering dream that now seemed to come to her most nights. It was as if she could hear the calm voice even now. She closed her eyes and willed herself to remember. The faceless warrior promised her that soon, he would remove her from this horrible dungeon that she has been trapped in for so long. She would hear a clear, and calm voice saying, "I am coming, don't give up. I will set you free very soon. Just trust me." If only she could stay in that dream and never wake up, perhaps this nightmare would end.

Every time that she heard that voice, she wished that someone would take her out of her misery. She didn't care how she just didn't want it to continue. How long can a person be locked up in a dungeon and beaten? She believed each day that she would not last another day, her body would shut down from the pain. Surely, she imagined this voice and this dream because of the pain.

Hearing the clang of metal doors, Keela instantly awoke. The memory of last night's dream immediately gone. The sound of metal dungeon doors slamming only meant one thing. The man whom the king called Philip, the same soldier who had captured her, would be coming for her. He would drag her out to the next room where the king would demand her to be punished again for something she still didn't understand.

Philip always seemed filled with anger and rage that seemed to consume him. Just his presence made Keela cringe. When he stood straight, he was six feet, three. Most of the time he walked slightly bent over with a heavy limp on his left side. He often cursed loudly and complained about the pain in his hip. His face had an ash grey color, and his black hair looked matted to the sides of his head.

As the dungeon door opened, a ripple of cruel laughter came from Philip's lips.

"What's the matter? You weren't hungry last night?"

He kicked the metal dish. Rats went scurrying across the floor. The clanging of the metal echoed against the stone walls.

"If you're not going to eat, then I am not going to waste the King's food! No more food for you for five days! That will teach you to be grateful!"

"I am sorry, I could not reach the food, please, I am hungry!" Keela begged.

"Yeah, sure you may be sorry now, but that is not going to change my mind. I could have eaten that perfectly good meal."

Today Keela noticed a second soldier standing a few feet behind Philip. He was a younger man, probably about five feet nine inches. Even in the shadowy darkness of the dungeon, he looked clean and well kept.

Philip came and stood directly in front of her. Instinctively, Keela backed away from Philip until her back pressed against the cold stone. Now, Philip stood inches from her face staring her in the eye. She refused to give this man pleasure in knowing that he intimidated her. Keela steeled herself against his gaze. His green eyes were so filled with rage. Keela felt the blood drain from her face. The smell of the alcohol on his breath made her head spin. *Focus, Keela ... Come on, he's just trying to scare you,* she thought to herself.

"Do you trust me?"

She heard those words so loudly, yet she knew she did not listen to them with her ears. *Where did I hear those words before?* She noticed the second soldier had stepped to the side slightly and intently watched her. *Did he say that?* She wondered, *no, I must be imagining things because of the pain. Yet, something about him seems familiar.*

Price of Freedom

Later that day, the second soldier came into her dungeon alone. She watched him as he came and stood just a few inches in front of her without saying a word. Cullen remembered the face of Queen Aideen. He took another look at the prisoner in front of him. *She is a mirror image of her mother! Surely this is Sine, the girl I am betrothed to.*

"I wish I could undo your chains right now and put salve on your wounds," He said.

Keela honesty believed he meant those words.

"I will get you out of here. You need to wait until the time is right."

"Do I know you?" Keela asked.

"Yes, we have met before. I will explain more after I have freed you from this prison. Right now, you must act as if you do not know me or Philip will suspect something. I must leave you now, but I will return. Do you trust me?"

His question about trust made Keela remember her dreams. She couldn't be dreaming It felt too painful to be a dream. Keela watched as the soldier walked from the dungeon and locked the door again. Why did she think she had met him before? Suddenly she remembered his eyes. They were just like the eyes of the man she had spoken with at Mormhuir Cathair.

Once again, Philip took her from the cell and with her hands tied securely behind her back. He practically dragged her down the hall to meet with King Dorcha. As she entered the room, she noticed the second soldier standing to the right of Dorcha. He had never been ordered to punish her before today.

"I'll ask you again," Dorcha started. "What weapon do you have to defeat me?"

"My lord," she said, her voice quivering. "I do not know of this weapon you are asking me for."

"Nonsense!" He yelled standing up from his chair. "It has been foretold that you and your husband shall defeat me! That can only happen with a weapon!" Dorcha face was turning red with anger. "Who is your husband?!"

Frustrated, Keela said "Why do you keep asking me the same question? I have no husband!" Philip knocked her so hard in the back of her head that she fell to her knees.

"Bow before the king and speak to him with the respect he deserves!" Philip sneered.

Too dizzy to stand, she remained kneeling before the king, only staring at the dirt floor. If she tried to get up, Philip would merely push her down again.

"My lord," Keela heard the voice of the second soldier. "Will you let her go free if I give you King Cullen, your greatest enemy?"

The tension in the room was so tangible, the hairs on the back of her neck stood up. Keela dared not to move. She glanced up at Dorcha. His mouth, slightly open as he thought about the offer. Then he and Philip began to roar with laughter. Once the laughter stopped, he said,

"Are you having compassion for this girl?" He chuckled, "How would you ever get me, King Cullen?"

"You did not answer my question, my lord." the soldier said without wavering.

"Of course, I would let her go if I had Cullen to punish instead. I give you my word. However, I know you will never be able to capture Cullen and bring him to me." Dorcha said with a chuckle, "So, let me continue interrogating this prisoner."

After those words, the second soldier removed his helmet and leather armor. "I am King Cullen." He said as he stood and looked Dorcha directly in the eyes. "Now let her go."

Keela couldn't believe her ears. *Why would he do such a thing? Doesn't he know that this horrible man would just kill him? They would never let me go free!* The thought of the punishment that this man was willing to take on her behalf made her sick to her stomach.

Dorcha looked shocked for a moment but quickly recovered. Keela couldn't tell if his voice sounded afraid or just angry. "Cullen?! Why would you care for this beggar?"

Cullen did not say a word.

"Cullen, I asked you a question!" Dorcha's anger was mounting. Still, Cullen did not say a word.

"Fine!" Dorcha shouted. "I'll let her go free after you have paid the price for her freedom." He gave a cruel laugh that made Keela's skin crawl. The King waved his hand in her direction, "Take her back to her dungeon cell. You better say goodbye to her now, you won't have a chance later!"

Silently, Cullen turned toward Keela. "Come," he said as he led her by the hand.

As he walked her back to her dungeon, Keela could hear Dorcha and Philip roaring with laughter. The sound of the chilling laughter echoed against the cold hard stone. The questions that had been swirling in Keela's mind were now screaming in her ears. She couldn't stay quiet any longer.

"Why did you do that for me? Don't you know what they will do to you?! Don't you realize they just plan on killing you? Run! Get out of here! Forget about me. This is my problem, not yours!"

Cullen turned and looked straight into her eyes, the tenderness she saw startled her.

"I know, but I am not about to leave you here and forget about you. Your more precious to me than anything Dorcha can do to me."

"What?!? Why would ...?" She stammered, "You don't even know me!"

"I know you much more than you realize. I have known you since you were a young child."

Again, Keela could not get over the look of love in this man's eyes. "But, that's impossible, because I never met you before Mormhuir Cathair."

"You have met me; you just don't remember," he said quietly.

Keela's mind raced. *Even if he did know me that well, why would he risk his own life for me? He must know I am nothing special.*

"That doesn't answer my question. Don't you know what Dorcha will do to you? They will probably kill you, and I'll still be stuck here in this dungeon." Keela's voice could not hide the fear and frustration rising in her heart.

"My love for you is stronger than death; I know what I am doing, do you trust me?"

Keela could not bring herself to say the words that she was thinking. *How am I supposed to trust him now?*

Cullen continued, "I will come back for you. Please believe this is true."

Again, he gazed steadily into her eyes. His eyes were sad, yet somehow still tender towards her, and she realized he was fully aware what he chose to do.

"Trust me; you are now free. Dorcha and Philip can no longer hurt you."

After he said those words, he gave her a tender, lingering kiss. Once again, he looked her in the eye and said, "Trust me; this is the only way." He held her gaze which to Keela felt like an eternity. Turning, he walked out of her dungeon cell, leaving the door wide open.

Cullen braced himself for what was coming next. He knew the only way to get Keela free from the wicked king's grasp was to take the punishment on himself. It would not be an easy task, but it was the only way. As he entered the room, Philip grabbed Cullen and held him firmly with Cullen's arms behind his back.

"You are a stupid man if you thought I would let you go!" Dorcha shouted, "I have waited years for this day."

Cullen gave no comment.

"Let's start this punishment with a good whipping. Forty lashes with a bone laced whip should do you some good." Dorcha chuckled.

Dorcha watched as his Philip carried out his orders. He got great pleasure watching this torture. Dorcha began envisioning the attack Philip would head up to conquer Dia Richoet. First, he would order all the soldiers who deserted to be captured. They would force them into the street along with their wives and children and have them all killed making an example out of all of them.

Once Cullen endured the forty lashes, several men began hitting him with clubs as they mocked him and spit on him. Cullen could no longer stand, he stumbled and fell to the ground at the feet of Philip.

"As for the girl, we will have our way with her when you're gone. You may have paid the price to set her free, but she will never know how to get away from us. Get up!"

Cullen was pulled to his feet by the other soldiers. His face, so severely beaten, his eyes were dark purple and swollen he could barely open them. Cullen didn't even have the strength to wipe the blood from his brow.

Dorcha stood watching, his emotions in turmoil. His feelings were mixed with anger and misery.

"Look, he's barely recognizable as the man who once stood strong, ready to take that tramp's place."

All the soldiers laughed at Dorcha's comment. For some reason, instead of feeling happy watching this torture, he became enraged. *Why did I give him my word and let the girl free? Cullen would never know I didn't keep my word if he's dead. I have waited my whole life for this moment,* Dorcha thought to himself, *why isn't Cullen even trying to fight back?*

Philip grew tired of this torture. Swiftly he pulled the dagger from his belt and plunged it into Cullen's side. Blood and water gushed from Cullen's side. Cullen sank to his knees still refusing to cry out in pain. Through the agonizing pain, Cullen struggled to get just another breath, as darkness filled his senses. Closing his swollen eyes, he imagined Sine's face. She was the only reason Cullen allowed this to happen. He would never regret setting her free from the chains that held her for so long. Once Philip knew Cullen was dead, they dragged his body to the mound of trash outside the city.

Keela stood in her prison cell. She heard the doors open down the hall. *Could this be Cullen?* She held her breath hoping that maybe he did survive. Her heart sank as she saw … Philip.

"Well, that's over and done with he laughed. I haven't had that much fun in a long time."

He gave a cruel laugh as he looked at Keela. Those green beady eyes, filled with mocking laughter, gave her a chill down to her soul.

"He's never coming back for you." he chuckled. "I made sure of that. So, you're free to walk out of your dungeon if you can get past me. I will keep my word; the door is open it will stay that way."

Keela started to step forward, but Philip charged at her.

"I said, you have to get past me! You don't think I will simply let you just walk out of here now do you?!"

Fear gripped her heart. "But Cullen paid for my freedom, let me go!"

"As I said, you will have to get past me. You're free, can't you see the prison cell is left wide open just like Cullen left it. Go ahead. I dare you. Leave!"

Keela sank to the floor and wept. Cullen had paid for her freedom, but she still was not free. *Why did he allow himself to be beaten and killed for me? What did Cullen mean when he said, 'I have known you since you were a young child.'? That's impossible! Didn't he know that loving me was pointless if he was dead? What good does that kind of love do anyway?*

Keela continued to weep for the loss of a love that she couldn't even understand, a love that knew no fear. Hearing the scoffing ridicule that Philip gave her, Keela didn't care that she was lying on the floor with the rats and the filth she had no energy to pick herself up and rest on the bench in her prison cell. She wept until exhaustion took over her body and she slept lying on the floor.

Just as the legend stated; three days after Cullen paid the price for the women's freedom, pure love gave his life back to him. He stood, feeling healthy and full of life. The markings from the beatings and the gash from Philips knife were still very evident, yet the pain was gone. Determined, He headed back to the dungeon to make sure Dorcha kept his word.

It had been three days, and Keela hadn't eaten a thing. She had no desire to do anything. Daily, Philip told her the horrible details of just how he killed Cullen and how much he enjoyed doing it. Keela wished she could just curl up on the floor and die, the shock and pain knowing what happened to Cullen was more than she could bear. Philip threw his insults and laughter at her all day. Continually laughing and telling her how stupid Cullen was to ever fall in love with someone as worthless as she was.

"You know you're a nobody right? Nobody cares that you're in here, no one will ever even know. I guess the only one who knew or cared is gone. Your only purpose in life is to keep me company. Maybe someday, I'll let you out of here, but only if you become my wife. Then I'll keep you where a woman belongs," he sneered.

Philip had not noticed Cullen as he stepped into the doorway. Cullen looked at Keela, his love. She was crouched down in the corner of her cell, with her hands over her face, her fingers covered her eyes, and her thumbs were pressed into her ears trying to block out Philips' words. Anger rose in Cullen's heart. Philip had no right to talk to her like that. Swiftly, Cullen stepped into the room directly in front of Philip and said,

"You have no right speaking to her like that. I paid for her freedom. You will let her walk from this room a free woman. You will not speak another word to her."

Keela sat cowering in the corner of her cell, blocking her ears with both hands. Oh, how she wanted to forget the sound of Philips' haunting laughter. Suddenly, his laughter stopped short. Silence took its place. She could sense someone had walked into the room. After a few seconds of silence, she peered through her fingers to see what had stopped Philip's cruel laughter. What she saw made her heart skip a beat.

A man had walked in and stood between her and Philip. *Was that Cullen? Did he come back for me? No, Philip told me over and over again that Cullen was dead.* She wished the man would turn around and look at her, but he had his back to her, facing Philip. Philip's face was whiter than as she had ever seen. His unblinking eyes wide open in unbelief looked more like round saucers. His jaw hung open as if someone had taken the very breath from his lungs and he had no power to move. Keela heard a voice that was so low and quiet that she couldn't make out what was said or who said it, but Philip barely nodded his head in agreement.

Cullen walked up to Keela and helped her stand to her feet. She was violently trembling from head to toe.

"H-H How? They told me you were dead!" She stammered.

"I told you my love was greater than death. Didn't you hear my words?" He said with a smile.

"I heard them; I just didn't understand them."

"It was foretold that if I freely laid down my life, for the sake of love. No man could take it from me. That's why I said love is stronger than death." Cullen took her into his arms and embraced her. "Let's go; you are free to walk out of this prison cell."

"But, I don't think I can."

"Why not? No chains are holding you back."

"I am not strong enough. I can't walk past Philip or the other guards."

"They are powerless, don't worry. Your enemy may look scary, but I am right here. I'll help you walk past them."

Keela's mind was racing. Cullen still had the scars and wounds from the punishment that he had taken for her. How could he be strong enough to walk never mind help her!

Cullen did not say another word, but carefully placed his arm around her waist avoiding her wounds and slowly walked her past Philip who was still staring as if he was a dead man. They continued to walk past the other cells and out into the courtyard. The sun was shining, and people were happy and carried on with their daily lives as if Cullen and Keela weren't even there. Keela felt like she was invisible. Why didn't anyone notice the two of them? They should be staring at the wounds and scars. Maybe offer to help or try to catch them thinking they were criminals. She waited for this dream to stop and she would wake up. The farther they walked, the fewer people she noticed. Keela looked up into the blue eyes of Cullen. He was gently leading her out of the city. His eyes sparkled in the light of day as if he had just gotten the most precious treasure he could have.

Safe Haven

Cullen could not get over the feeling in his heart. He had done it! Now Sine was free, and they were walking out the dungeon cell together. He understood that Keela was shocked and she didn't understand. She needed time to appreciate his love for her. Cullen knew that he needed to be patient and loving as he waited for her to understand.

Right now, there were more important things on his mind. Keelas' wounds were evident. She wore a ragged, torn dress. Her back was partially exposed, and Cullen could see the stripes on her back from the last beating she endured. Her legs gave way with weakness as they walked. She was not ready to travel great distances. Instead, she needed a safe place to stay. A place where he could nurse her back to health without any enemy being able to find them. He was sure that Philip or some other soldiers would be out looking for them soon. Cullen knew just the place he would take her. Many times, he traveled with his father into the forest that bordered King Dorcha's kingdom. Cullen recalled the day he accidentally found the safe haven he was going to take Sine to. The memory came to his mind as if it happened just yesterday.

Cullen and his father had been traveling. They had grown weary from the long travel, and the horses needed a drink of water. Cullen's father, King Domnall, stopped at a beautiful clear lake. A fast-flowing waterfall plummeted off a high cliff. His father dismounted and lightened the horses' loads to allow them to rest and to let them get a refreshing drink. Cullen begged his father to let him swim. The fresh water would revive him. Reluctantly, his father allowed him to, but only for a few minutes.

His father turned his back toward him as he took care of the horses. Cullen wanted to get as close as he could to the waterfall. He could still remember how refreshing and crisp the water felt. He waded into the water careful not to wade in too deep. The cascading water mesmerized him. *If only I can reach just a little farther, I will be able to touch the waterfall,* he thought to himself. The crashing waterfall roared so loudly in his ears; he did not hear his father yelling for him to come to shore.

Cautiously, he took one more step out. Cullen could not regain his footing, as the rock, he stood on toppled over. Each time he tried to stand, his feet slid on the moss-covered rocks. Cullen, still a young boy, could not swim well. Panic began to fill his mind.

"Father!" he shouted as loud as he could, "Help me!"

No matter how hard he tried to swim, the current began dragging him toward the raging waterfall.

"Father!"

His second cry could not be heard as his head went under the water. Again, and again, he struggled to swim to the surface. Further and further he sank under the force of the raging waterfall. His lungs were screaming for air as the current of the water pushed him against the hard stones that created this gorge under the waterfall. As his hands groped along the rocks, he discovered an opening under the water.

When he swam into the opening, his head surfaced. Relief flooded his mind as he gasped for air. He climbed into the cave and stood to his feet. He saw the ceiling of the cave, high enough that a full-grown man could stand straight without hitting his head. Light emanated from the left side. As he walked to the opening, he saw sunlight shining through a canopy of trees high above him with lush growth with berry bushes scattered before him.

Cullen knew that his father must be worried sick about him. *How can I get out of the cave? I'm not strong enough to swim against that current,* He thought. Screaming at the top of his lungs, he called for his father until he had no voice left. No matter how hard he yelled, his father would not be able to hear him above the roar of the waterfall. He watched the light fade in the canopy area. *Father, please find me!* He thought to himself as he sat on the floor of the cave. Slowly the tears came as darkness filled the cavern.

King Domnall was strong and brave with a determination to do whatever it took to protect his family, especially his only son. He loved his son with an unearthly kind of love and would not stop looking until he found Cullen. His love for his son is stronger than anyone had seen a man love a son. Cullen remembered the joy that he felt when he woke up and saw his father standing over him. The concern in his father's eyes made Cullen feel guilty for scaring him, yet he couldn't believe that his father found him. *Am I dreaming?* He thought. Hoarse from calling for his father, his voice sounded more like a whisper.

"Father?"

"Yes, Cullen, I am right here." Cullen shook his head and the memory cleared.

Keela couldn't believe that Cullen could be walking. Her wounds from the whipping that she received several days ago was enough to drive her out of her mind. Cullen seemed to know when Keela's strength was failing; he always caught and held her securely each time she stumbled. As they approached a field, Keela saw the horse. Panic filled her heart. *I can't ride that horse!* She thought to herself, *I don't know how to ride, and even if I did, I am sure my pain would not allow me to jump up and mount a horse.*

"I can't," she started to say. Cullen stopped her short.

"Do you trust me?"

Why did he always say that to her? She tried to trust him, but her fears were stronger. "I'm trying," she said quietly.

Cullen smiled at her, "I know you're scared."

As they approached the horse, Cullen instructed her to hold on to his neck. He held her legs in his left arm and mounted his horse only using his free arm and his legs. Cullen placed her across Hunter's withers so he could have two free hands to steer. Keela didn't want to let go. She would fall off the horse for sure if she tried to sit by herself. As she sat with her arms wrapped around Cullen's neck, she rested her head against his shoulder. It seemed like the most comfortable thing to do. Soon she felt herself nodding off to sleep with the rhythmic pace of Hunter's gentle gait.

Keela must have fallen asleep for a short while. She woke to feel the pounding of the horse's hooves on the ground below. Hunter was moving very fast now. Cullen had his right arm wrapped around her shoulders, holding her tightly to his chest. How long had she fallen asleep? As she stirred, Cullen looked down at her and grinned. He kissed the top of her head and said

"Good morning, beautiful! Sorry to wake you."

Keela was surprised by his comment, "Beautiful?!" she laughed. "Ha! I am not a sight of beauty right now. I have ripped clothes, my hair is filthy, and I haven't been able to brush out the knots in forever. Not to mention I need to wash. I'm certainly not beautiful."

Keela felt the heat rise in her face as she realized how she must have sounded. Cullen slowed the horse down to a slow walking speed. He looked down into her face a gently pushed a rebellious wisp of hair from her face.

"Oh, but you are to me. The beauty that I see and long for is not always just your outward appearance. It's your heart."

Keela was sure she was filthy inside and out. Her old happy, confident attitude was gone. How disappointing for poor Cullen, she wasn't who he thought she was. She was wasted and useless. Everyone told her that, so why would she believe any differently. For so long now, she was convinced that she was hopeless to everyone who came in contact with her, that is until she met Cullen.

Cullen was expecting Keela to refuse his compliment. He

meant every word. His love for her was far more than her outward appearance. He knew her happy, cheerful personality. The one that had been pulled down by the situations and circumstances around her, but he knew it was still there. Cullen remembered the happy child he once knew before her parents locked her away in the convent with the nuns for protection. He recalled the self-confidence and boldness she had when he saw her trading her vegetables in the seaport village. Her confidence that she would be alright living in the field without a place to call home and not enough money to buy food to fill her stomach. He ached for that day. Why didn't he take her home with him then? He knew his answer. She would never have come with him, and he had not recognized who she was. She had been on his mind ever since that day. Another question that plagued his thoughts was, *Why was she going around calling herself Keela?* When Dorcha questioned her, she said that she did not know about her parents. Is it true she doesn't even remember her real identity? It would take some time, but he would help her remember her past. Her parents were amazing, loving parents. They were king and queen of a great kingdom. If war did not break out in the country, and her parents did not die, things would have been so different for the girl. Cullen scanned the horizon. He headed towards the woods and the safe haven where he would take Sine to until she was strong enough to travel great distances.

Marcus was looking out over the cliffs toward the ocean. His heart was frustrated that his wife has seemed to change her attitude ever since his son Ronan was born. Moria was angry almost all the time. Marcus figured that all the new responsibilities of having a newborn son must be weighing on her, but why would she take it out on him? He was only trying to help. Just last night she lashed out at him again. Thinking Moria might like a hand with cooking dinner, Marcus came into the kitchen to see what he could do to help her.

"What do you need me to do?" he asked.

Her reply cut him like a knife. "Do you think I can't do my job or something? Why would I need your help? I am fully capable of making dinner myself." She hesitated for a moment, and Marcus thought perhaps she would apologize for her comment. Instead, she said, "Hey, I am trying as hard as I can to take care of your son, clean your house and cook food for you. If I am suddenly not good enough for you, just leave. I'm sure someone else would be happy to do all your commands."

What had happened to his beautiful Moria? She used to be so free, just being around her would make him feel alive. She always knew what to do to make him smile or even laugh when things were going bad. He remembered the first time he met Moria. She willingly tended to his needs every day. Feeding him and gently cleaning his wounds and replacing his bandages. When Marcus was strong enough to sit up and enjoy company, Moria did not leave his side. Instead, she became his best companion. Moria would tell him all the happenings of the kingdom. She would keep him updated with the news of the fighting that continued in the South. Most of all, she would do little things just to make him smile. He shook his head. *When did all that change and why did it change? I still adore her, but does she still love me?*

Do you trust me?

Keela wondered why they were going into the forest again. Once the undergrowth of the forest became too thick, Cullen dismounted Hunter leaving Keela to sit by herself. Silently, he led hunter through the dense vegetation of the forest. Keela had not spoken a word. She was haunted by her memories of the first time she traveled in the woods. Fear was tugging at her heart. The forest plant life was dense, and the thick fog gave everything a strange appearance.

"Where are we going?" She asked.

Cullen did not answer or even look at her. Keela felt as if her heart was lodged in her throat making it difficult to swallow. Still, Cullen had not said a word, he just led the horse along a seemingly invisible path. Keela's hands trembled as she held tightly to Hunter's mane. She felt as if she would suddenly burst into tears. *What is wrong with me?* She wondered to herself. *Why won't he talk to me?*

Cullen heard Keela ask where they were going, and he noticed her voice trembled as she spoke. *She needs to learn to trust me,* he thought to himself, *I am not always going to calm her fears by telling her every time she gets scared that it's going to be alright.* Cullen knew there would be times when she would need to believe his love for her even if he did not reassure her. He continued to walk in silence. Keela did not question him further which Cullen was grateful for. Her silence told him that she was trying to trust him even though he did not acknowledge her fears.

After they had traveled a short distance into the woods, the fog began to lift. The sun was penetrating through the fog giving the area a bright look. Keela was squinting from the brightness of the mist. As Cullen turned Hunter to the right, they began to climb a steep hill leaving the fog behind in the valley. Once they reached the top of the peak, the terrain was again flat and still dense with the forest growth. The tall cedar trees looked as if they stretched to the sky. Keela could not see the tops of the trees, but she noticed that there was no sign of the dense fog that had recently covered the forest floor.

Off in the distance, the roar of rushing water could be heard. Keela did not see any sign of water, and she could not tell which direction the sound was coming from. Cullen was gently pushing the forest undergrowth to the side to create a path for Hunter. Soon Keela noticed a range of sheer rock cliffs come into view. The height of these cliffs was breathtaking. *That must be where the water is coming from,* she thought. As they walked toward the cliffs, Keela could see the rushing waterfall. It fell from the top of the cliffs into a large lake. The lake was large enough that despite the waterfall, the shore water was very peaceful and calm. Cullen led Hunter to the edge of the water and reached up to gently help Keela off the horse.

Keela carefully dismounted Hunter. She was still in intense pain, but she welcomed the thought of getting off the horse even for a short while. Her wounds on her back were still very raw and open. Each time she moved she was reminded of her past. Her enemies, and the fact that she still had no idea why people were so against her. Even though Keela was very scared of the forest just moments ago, she was filled with an indescribable peace. She looked at Cullen as he was removing the saddle from Hunter. *What is it about him that makes me feel so safe and protected?* She wondered, *I know he cares about me, but why?* Again, the thoughts in her mind kept telling her that she was not good enough to be treated so lovingly. Soon Keela forgot about the peace she was feeling, and frustration took hold of her mind. Just then, Cullen turned toward her.

"How are you doing?"

"Well, I am hurting all over, my back is killing me, I feel so filthy, I am hungry and tired. How do you think I am doing?" Keela complained. Keela was surprised at her own response. Looking at the ground, she shuffled her feet in the pebbles along the shore. "I-I-I am sorry," She whispered. "I didn't mean to sound so ungrateful. It's just that I am still in a lot of pain and I keep thinking that it's all a dream."

Cullen smiled a genuine smile. "It's ok; I understand what you're feeling." The look on his face became more intense, but his eyes held a gentleness that felt like a caress to her soul. "Keela, do you trust me?"

Keela was taken aback by the question. *How can I trust someone I barely know?* She thought, *but he has already shown me that he is worthy of my trust. Why is this so difficult for me?* She looked at Cullen; his eyes were willing her to believe him.

"I am trying," she said, her voice barely a whisper.

Cullen didn't try to hide the disappointment as he thought to himself. *Why won't she trust me? After all, I have done for her? How long must I wait before she believes me?* Instead, he smiled and said, "You will learn to trust me more and more each day. It's crucial that you trust me with everything."

"I will try, please don't be upset with me, it's just that I have had so many people fail me it's hard to trust. Most people have only been there for a short while, and then they end up hurting me some way," Keela thought back to the nuns who raised her. Even they deserted her and walked away as if she never meant more to them than a passing of time.

As Keela looked up again, she noticed Cullen was intently watching her, "I have a safe haven I want to bring you to, but you must trust me with your life."

Keela's breath caught in her throat. "What do you mean? You scare me when you talk like that."

Cullen put his hand on her shoulder and said, "There is nothing to be afraid of. I will not let you fail. You just need to trust me."

Keela was getting frustrated. *Why does he always have to bring it back to this whole trust issue? Doesn't he understand that I can't trust?*

What does it matter if I do or not? By the look on his face, Keela knew that he would not do another thing until she told him that she indeed did trust him. Hoping that her real feelings were not showing on her face. She quietly mumbled, "Ok, I trust you."

Cullen's eyes lit up with a great smile, "Good, come with me."

Cullen could tell that Keela struggled with the whole idea of trusting him. He knew and understood that in time, he would ultimately earn her trust. Right now, she was trying her best to trust him, that was enough for him. He walked Keela to the side of the lake. Slowly he walked her into the lake until she was up to her knees in the cold, water. The water was so clear that it was easy to see the bottom. After a moment, he led her into the deeper water. With the sun on her face, Keela closed her eyes and smiled. Cullen watched her, the smile on her face made it clear that the water was a relief and a pleasure for her.

With her eyes still closed, she said, "I wish I learned how to swim when I was a girl; I think I would love to dive into this lake and let the cool water soothe my wounds."

Cullen smiled. "That's exactly what we are going to do."

Panic seized her heart instantly. Now her eyes were wide with fear. "No!! Please! I can't swim!" She begged.

The fear that emanated from her eyes made Cullen's heart hurt. "I know you can't swim. I thought you said you would trust me?"

"Well, I didn't know you were talking about swimming!" she shrieked.

"Listen carefully to what I am about to say, Keela. I know you can't swim. I already figured out how to take care of that problem. We need to swim to get to the safe haven I have picked out for you."

"How have you already figured out that problem?"

"Just trust me and wait and see."

Carefully, Cullen walked Keela out into the deeper water. When the water was up to her chin, he turned toward her. Keela had not said a word, but her expression plainly showed her fear.

"I am trying very hard to trust you," Keela whispered in a shaky voice.

"Good, I promise I won't let you down," Cullen said with a smile. Carefully he took a soft cloth from his pocket. "Now, I will cover your nose, so you won't accidentally inhale any water. Okay?"

Keela barely nodded. Tears were burning her eyes, but she willed herself not to cry. *Come on Keela, you need to trust him,* she thought. After he had tied the cloth around her nose, he tied another, very loosely from her chin to the top of her head.

"You may open your mouth to breath, but when we go underwater, I will tighten the sash around your chin, so you don't swallow any water. Okay?"

Keela again nodded this time the tears in her eyes slipped down her cheeks. Cullen gently wiped the tear away with his thumb.

"Keela, I promise, it will be ok."

Slowly, Cullen turned so he stood back to back with her and as gently as possible, he wrapped a rope around her shoulder under her arms and across his chest. He could feel her trembling with fear.

"Ok, Keela, you need to just relax and let me do the swimming. If you fight me, things will be much more difficult for both of us. Please promise me that you will continue to trust me and not panic."

Keela nodded her head as the tears continued to silently flow down her face. Keela could feel herself trembling. She wanted to trust him, but everything about her was panicking. *This is crazy!* She thought to herself.

Cullen began swimming toward the waterfall. Keela was trying her hardest not to think about what was happening. She could feel Cullen's strength as he swam with confidence. *Why are we heading straight toward the waterfall? Oh yeah, remember, you're not supposed to panic. ...* Every once in a while, she wanted to panic, but she kept trying to resist the urge to fight against the rope that held her securely to Cullen as he swam. Cullen stopped swimming for a minute, just long enough to say,

"Okay, we are going to go under for a little while. Take a deep breath."

Keela took a shaky breath and then felt the cloth gently tighten around her head just like Cullen told her he would do. As the cold water covered her, she concentrated on the sensation the water gave her wounds; it felt wonderful. Almost like it was cleaning and healing her wounds. She no longer felt filthy. Soon, her lungs began to burn, and she wanted to scream for air. *How long is he going to stay underwater?* She thought. As fear again threatened to fill her senses. He was still swimming in a downward fashion. Slowly, blackness came over Keela, and she fell into a deep sleep.

Cullen was swimming as hard as he could, hoping Keela would not begin to panic. He felt the tension in Keela's body as they started swimming. He especially felt her tighten as he told her they were going underwater. However, he was surprised at the way she relaxed as they first started going under. After they had been underwater for a short time, he felt her whole body become rigid. Almost like she was panicking. Cullen knew that meant her lungs were burning for air. He was almost to the opening of the safe haven. Would she hold out long enough for him to show her the safe haven that was waiting for here? Feeling her body go completely limp, Cullen knew that she had passed out. Within seconds, he surfaced in the cave. Immediately, he reached up and untied the cloth that had held her mouth firmly closed and the second cloth that had been covering her nose so she could not inhale. Instantly, she began to breathe. However, she was still unconscious. Cullen untied the rope that had kept her fastened to his back. Carefully, he picked her up out of the water. Walking a short distance, he gently placed her on the bed he had prepared from the furs of animals that he previously hunted. Cullen stepped back and studied Keela. She was breathing normally he could tell by the gentle rise and fall of her chest, but she had not woken. Knowing that Sine would be fine, Cullen set out to find some food. He knew she would be hungry when she awoke.

Healing coming / New Garment

Keela woke up and opened her eyes. The first thing she saw was a high stone ceiling. The stone had a smooth, worn appearance. Keela turned her head to the right. *I wonder what's over there?* She thought. The questions began swirling in her mind. *Where am I? Am I dreaming? No, we were swimming. How did Cullen get me here? Why didn't I drown?* The last thing she remembered was panicking because she needed air and needed it now! She strained her eyes looking in every corner of the cave searching for Cullen. She did not see anyone anywhere. *He wouldn't have left her here alone.* She thought to herself trying to keep calm. *No, he wanted me to trust him. I'm sure he didn't desert me now.* She was laying on a very soft bed made up of many furs. Too tired to get up and look around, she drifted back into a peaceful sleep.

Keela awoke to the sound of a fire crackling. She opened her eyes and saw Cullen in the far corner of the cave. He was mixing something in an empty turtle shell that he was using as a bowl. Next to him was a piece of meat cooking over the fire. Cullen seemed to know when she woke up.

He turned to her and said, "How are you feeling now?"

Keela let that question sit in her mind for a few moments. She remembered what her answer was last time he had asked that question

'Well, I am hurting all over, my back is killing me, I feel so filthy, I am hungry and tired. How do you think I am doing?' As she remembered those words, heat rose in her cheeks. Keela was embarrassed by the way she had treated him earlier. She didn't want to complain similar to last time, so she gave it some thought. Keela soon realized that she did not feel filthy anymore. Her wounds felt clean, and she was not as tired.

"I am actually feeling a bit better than I was just the other day."

"Good" Cullen stood and walked across the cave with the bowl in his hands. "Now, I would like you to sit up and let me put this on your wounds on your back.

Keela didn't want to move. *I can't let him see my wounds!* She thought. *Why can't he just leave them alone? They will eventually heal, right?*

"I don't know about that," she mumbled, "I am fine, really. I don't need any help."

Cullen chuckled, but the smile emanating from his eyes plainly told her that he was not laughing at her.

"Keela," he said with a smile, "I already know about the wounds that you have endured. Remember, I only want what is best for you, and right now, you need this healing balm put on your wounds. If you don't take care of these past hurts, they will only fester and hurt you more."

She was afraid that sticky stuff was going to hurt like crazy. "Please, I can't take any more pain. I'm sure those herbs will make it hurt more. I can't …"

Cullen interrupted her "Keela; I thought you trusted me. I know what I am doing. This is for your own good. Please let me help you."

For reasons she didn't understand, she agreed. Her garment was already tattered and shredded from the whipping that she received, so there was no hiding the fact that the injury was there. Keela sat up and turned her open back toward Cullen. Steeling herself against the pain that was bound to come as he applied the healing balm.

Cullen wanted to cry when he looked at her wounds. She was a brave woman to have endured this; he knew that for sure. He loved her so much, and someday, he would get revenge on the people who had hurt the woman he loved. There was no question in his mind. They would answer to him, and nothing was going to take his wrath away. He took in a shaky breath, now was not the time to think about that. Right now, he needed to help her regain her strength. He began to apply the healing balm that he had made from different herbs in the area. As he gently spread the ointment across her back, he was glad to see that her body began to relax under his touch. Healing was soon to come.

Keela was shocked to feel all the pain leave her back as he began to spread on the healing balm. It was bringing a sensation that took all her pain away. Again, she wondered what was it about Cullen; he could bring peace into almost every situation. It almost felt like he was spreading peace across her soul as he applied the balm to her back. After Cullen had applied the ointment to her wounds, Keela laid on her stomach on the bed to allow the medicine to dry on her back.

"Try to sleep, I will be back in a few minutes," she heard Cullen say. Soon she felt herself begin to drift off to sleep.

When Keela woke, she felt as if she had slept for several hours. She could smell food cooking and hear Cullen near her. As she tried to sit up, Cullen immediately came to her side.

"Here, let me help you," he said, as he gently helped her to a sitting position, "Glad you were able to sleep." Cullen returned to the fire and stirred the food that was cooking. "Keela, I have a new garment I want you to wear. It's a garment I made for you."

Keela was grateful for the idea of wearing a new robe instead of the tattered one she had on. When Cullen turned and showed her the garment he had made, she was breathless.

"Cullen! It is beautiful!"

Cullen smiled, "I'm glad you like it, please, put it on."

Cullen turned and walked into another part of the cave to give her privacy to change her filthy garment for the new one he had just given her.

After she put on the new garment, she sat and admired it. The seamless garment appeared so white it seemed to glimmer in its own light. The hood and long sleeves would help keep her warm in cold weather, and it was her exact length. It came just to the floor, yet it did not drag in the dirt. The feeling of the smooth silk on her skin was like a gentle caress which seemed to soothe her wounds. Keela did not notice Cullen walking back to her and was startled when she heard his voice.

"Well, I take it by your expression, you like it."

Keela turned to see Cullen standing leaning against the wall of the cave, "Yes! It is beautiful, and it feels wonderful!" she said. "How did you make it so perfect?"

Cullen smiled, "Well, I wanted it to be perfect for you." He left his spot near the cave wall where he was standing and came toward Keela. "It sure brings out the beauty in your eyes. This is much better than that filthy, torn garment you were wearing for so long."

Now that Cullen was closer, Keela couldn't help but notice the sparkle in Cullen's eye. *Do I really make him that happy?* She wondered.

"Thank You, Cullen. This means more to me than you may realize."

"No," Cullen said, "This garment means a lot more than you realize. It tells everyone that you belong to me. It doesn't matter what you have already gone through with your enemies; people shouldn't care about where you came from or who you were. The truth is, this garment shows them all that you're my bride."

Keela felt her mouth open, too stunned to speak for several minutes.

"Cullen, why?" she stammered. "Why would you love me like that? I am not lovable. You don't know the things I have been through!"

Cullen smiled, "I do love you like that."

Keela felt the tears begin to well up in her eyes. Somehow, she needed to convince him that she was not as good or as beautiful as he seemed to believe.

"You can't love me," Keela protested, "I am not good enough for someone like you."

Cullen held her at arm's length and gently caressed her arms, "Keela, please, don't think of yourself like that. I love you."

"But ..."

Cullen silenced her comment by placing his finger on her lips and said, "Keela, I love you more than you could ever understand and nothing you did or will do is going to change that, just accept my love."

Keela broke down and let the tears freely fall. For the first time in her life, she knew that she was truly loved. She didn't understand it, but she allowed herself to just believe it.

Safe Love

Several days had passed, and they were still staying in the safe-haven. Keela had begun to realize how much she looked up to Cullen. She never met anyone like him. What was it about him that made her want to stay with him forever? *Am I really finding love? I mean a pure kind of love?* Keela had all but given up on believing that love so pure could exist. She would want nothing better than to stay with him for the rest of her life. He clearly showed that he cared for her, but why? Keela still couldn't figure that out. What did she have that would even make a king like Cullen know she existed, never mind love her? She watched Cullen walk into the cave. He had come from the left where Keela saw the light coming from.

"What is over there?" Keela asked.

"Would you like to take a walk with me and see?"

Keela thought her strength was returning enough to take a short walk. "Yes! yes, I would like that very much."

Cullen came and helped her to her feet. "Good, I have wanted to share this with you since I brought you here."

Just the sound of his words made her heart beat a little faster. *What did he mean by that?* She wondered. They made their way slowly because she was still unsure on her feet. As they came to the end of the tunnel, Keela's breath caught in her throat.

"This is beautiful!" she whispered. "Cullen! How is this possible? I thought we were in a cave?"

Cullen watched Keela. Her mouth, slightly opened, and her eyes were wide in awe as she took in her surroundings. Those beautiful eyes that caught and captured his heart with just one glance were scanning the area in front of her. A smile played on his lips, "I am glad you like it."

"Like it? I love it! It's gorgeous. I thought you told me that we were underground? Like behind a waterfall or something."

Her bewildered look only made Cullen love her more. "Yes, we are underground. Yes, we are in a cave of sorts, and we are definitely under a waterfall." His smile told her that he knew all the questions that were running through her mind, but he didn't see them as foolish. "I found this safe haven many years ago with my father. I have stayed here many times since. You see, the waterfall is directly over the cave where you were staying. The only way into this safe haven is by swimming under the waterfall. At one time, I had climbed the steep banks of the cliffs until I came to the place the waterfall stems from. I saw the rushing river, and to the left a little ways, I could barely find the opening that creates this canopy where the light can filter its way into the cave, creating this protected area. No one can climb down the sides of the opening; they are very steep and smooth with no place to get a footing. The only way to enter is through swimming under the waterfall."

Keela seemed to be mesmerized by the sight of what lay in front of her. Along the cliff edge grew many fragrant cedar and cypress trees creating a green canopy. Here, on the ground were many different types of berry bushes and small plants. Birds were in abundance in this area, and the colors of the birds seemed more vibrant than any other bird that she had seen. The sweet fragrance filled the air with the scent of ripe fruit and flowers that spread out across the ground.

Cullen noticed that Keela was looking a little tired.

"Come, let's sit down and rest for a few minutes." He led Keela to a place where the flowers were growing like a lush carpet on the ground. Cullen picked a small basket of berries from the nearby bush and sat down. "Please, sit next to me."

The invitation couldn't have sounded better to her. Keela sat on the bed of flowers, her knees brought up to her chest as she wrapped her arms around her knees. She studied the birds and the flowers that surrounded her. *If only I could capture this moment and never leave. Life would be good for once,* she thought. She remembered the years before she had left the convent. *Things were different then. I wonder how Mother Sara and her sisters are. Do they ever even miss me?*

Cullen studied Sinc for a few moments. When he asked her to sit down next to him, he noticed that she kept her distance. She looked tired but happy. Sitting with her arms wrapped around her knees she looked timid and fragile. Her eyes were staring off into the distance, lost in thought. He understood that Keela did not want this moment to end. She did not want to face the world again. Every day he noticed her health returning, with that strength, he sensed her concern growing as well.

"What are you thinking?"

She seemed startled. "Nothing much, I was just trying to memorize the way I feel right now."

"Why do you want to memorize this moment?" he asked gently looking into her dark brown eyes. *Oh, how she had captivated his heart by just one glance of her eyes. Does she even realize that?* He wondered.

Keela suddenly seemed shy and timid. "Because if only things could stay this way, my life would be good for a little while, but I know we must move on, you are a king, and you have your kingdom to take care of." Her voice trailed off as she allowed herself to get lost in thought again.

"And you are afraid of that? Why?"

Keela looked embarrassed. "Sorry, I keep wondering what I will do when we get to your kingdom."

Cullen was grateful for her honesty. "We will still be together; I guarantee that will not change. I will never leave you as an orphan. Besides, I want you to be by my side in the throne room."

Keela glanced at him over her shoulder. "That all sounds nice, but it's not true," Keela said, staring at the grass at her feet and twisting a few blades of grass in her fingers. "I mean, I have nothing to offer you as far as your kingdom is concerned. I have no idea how to lead people, and you are far wiser than I ever would be."

Cullen chuckled, "Keela, you need to believe in yourself a little bit more."

Keela looked up to see Cullen smiling at her. "Wait and see," Keela said, "Soon you will realize I was right."

Cullen seemed frustrated with her comment but only said, "I can see your back is getting tired of sitting in that position. Come, sit against me. Put your head on my chest and just enjoy the time we have right now."

At first, she hesitated. She wasn't sure she wanted to allow that kind of intimacy. Slowly, Keela leaned up against him. She rested her head on his chest and listened to his heartbeat. The steady rhythm of his heartbeat gave her a sense of peace and strength. With every breath, she felt herself relax. He really did care, although Keela still didn't know why.

Keela turned herself slightly so she could see his face. Cullen looked down at Keela, the look of love shining clearly in his blue eyes. His smile spread across his face until it lit up his whole face. "What are you thinking?" he asked.

Keela wasn't sure what to say. She had so many questions, she didn't know where to start. *He said he knew me a long time ago, but how? When? How did he find me? Why does he love me? Was this love even real?* The whole story seemed so unreal to her that she almost didn't want to believe it. She didn't even know herself! Who were her parents and why did they give her to the convent?

"I just have a lot of questions in my mind, not sure what to think of anything right now. It all seems unreal."

Cullen smiled again. "Well, we have plenty of time to talk. What is it that you have questions about? I bet I can help answer some of those questions."

She leaned back on his chest taking in a deep breath of the fragrance of the flowers that were surrounding them. "Well, the first question I would have to ask would be how did you find me?" Keela listened to the beating of his heart for a few seconds before he spoke.

"Let me just say that you were calling out to me for help just about every night. I tried looking for you then, but I couldn't find you because you grew silent."

At those words, Keela jumped up and spun around to face him. The rapid movement made Keela feel dizzy. She grabbed onto a nearby branch to steady herself.

"Wait a minute; now you're more confusing! You mean I was calling out to you for help?!"

Cullen patted the ground next to him encouragingly. "Please sit back down."

Keela sat facing Cullen. She wanted to see the look in his eyes, he must be joking. As she gazed into his eyes, she saw only seriousness. What did he mean?

"Yes, actually you were calling out to me when you were scared or in pain. Each time I heard you, you were asleep. Like you were dreaming."

Cullen watched her expression. She had not said a word, yet Cullen could tell by the slight roll of her eyes that she did not believe a word that he had just said. Slowly her eyes got larger and her mouth opened as if to speak yet no words came. She realized the truth of what he had just said.

"I remember some of those dreams," she said in a hushed voice. Astonishment clearly marked on her face. "I thought I was losing my mind. I could hear a voice telling me that they were coming to help me. I never saw your face. Somehow in my dream, I always woke up with a little strength which made me feel like, I really could face another day. At least until you found me."

Cullen began to eat a few of the berries that he had picked. "Well, let me assure you that you were not losing your mind. We really were communicating through the dreams, but I never saw your face either. I could only tell about your surroundings. I must admit, I thought I came very close to finding you. I made my way to Mormhuir Cathair, and the dreams stopped. Now, I know we met. You were the woman at the marketplace. I bought carrots for my horse from you. I remember we talked a short while. You told me you had no place to call home. However, you were determined that you would be fine. Am I right?"

Just the expression on her face answered his question. Yes, he had met her in that little village. Oh, how he wished he could have turned time back to that day.

"Why did you stop talking to me? I am assuming that you just didn't think you needed my help anymore, right?" Keela nodded her head slowly.

If only she had known, that would have saved her a whole lot of heartache and pain. Only that following winter, she had been captured and beaten.

"Don't think about it Keela," Cullen said gently.

"Think about what?"

"You're regretting the past. I can see it in your face. There is nothing that you or I can do to change what already happened."

Keela looked at the ground. "No, maybe not, but still if only I had known. If only I had kept talking with you in my dreams, then you would have been able to find me." The frustration and deep regret growing deep in her heart felt like fingers threatening to choke her. "I wouldn't have been captured and beaten, and you never would have taken my punishment to set me free from King Dorcha."

Cullen chuckled quietly, the look of love clearly shining in his eyes. "Well, there would have always been a price to pay to get you as my own. No enemy of mine would ever have allowed me to just walk away with you. You're the most valuable treasure that I can have." The look of love in his eyes caught her by surprise.

"I guess that's another one of my questions. Why do you like me, never mind love me? What have I ever done? I am a nobody with nothing to offer ..."

Cullen put his finger to her lips to stop the next words. "My dear Keela, you may not realize your value or your self-worth, but that doesn't mean it isn't there. I don't love you for what you did, can do, or might do in the future. I love you for who you are, don't add anything, don't try to become someone you are not. I just love you. Please try to understand that."

Keela buried her face in her hands and cried. How can she understand this kind of love? She could hear the voices in her mind. *You know you're a nobody right? Nobody cares! You're useless, Stupid woman! You don't even know your own name! You will never amount to anything! You're a waste of my time.*

"Keela," Cullen said tenderly.

Hearing his voice made her want to run and hide, but she could not move. She could feel herself trembling as the sobs overtook her. Cullen pulled her close and gently caressed her head and shoulders. The more she thought about the words that were spoken to her, the more paralyzed she felt.

"Keela, it's okay, none of those words were true." Cullen continued to hold her rocking her gently as she cried. "You are the one I love. You are the one I would do anything for, including giving up my life. Your voice is like a sweet fragrance and your words melt my heart. You are the one I want to be with, the one I want to share my heart with."

As she rested in his loving embrace, the sobs slowly stopped, and peace filled her heart.

"I just don't understand it. I don't think I could ever understand why you love me." She leaned her head against his chest again. Exhausted from crying, she drifted off into a very peaceful sleep.

Trapped

Moria was home, taking care of the baby. *Does this ever end?* She thought. *Will I ever be myself again or am I now just part of this baby. I can't eat, sleep or even go anywhere without this baby strapped to my side. I love the baby very much, but since I had him, Marcus has gotten so busy he's never here. When he is here, all we do is argue. I feel like his little servant.* Moria was exhausted. Her newborn son just did not seem to get the idea of sleeping at night. Moria paced the small area in their living room trying to comfort the baby and keep him quiet so her husband Marcus could sleep. *Why should I care if Marcus is sleeping,* she thought. *Why doesn't he even try to help me take care of the baby so that I can get some sleep. He is so selfish! Sure, he has a big trip planned tomorrow but has he even noticed how exhausted I am.*

The more Moria thought about Marcus, the more upset she got. Her pace became faster as she walked around the room with the baby. *Why won't Ronan stop crying!* Tears filled her eyes. In all her life she never felt more taken advantage of. She felt like a slave to both her baby and her husband. Moria felt like a trapped animal. She would have run away from Marcus if she did not have a child to take care of. Now, with the baby, she felt trapped. I don't think I could make it on my own with a young child, and it's really not fair to the boy to raise him without a father.

Ronan's tears slowly subsided, Moria watched his face as he drifted off to sleep. It wasn't his fault that Moria was so miserable.

She studied his face. He sure looked a lot like his father. He had the same dark hair, the same eyes, and the same jawline that his father had. Sure, he had her nose and several of her expressions, but there was no escaping he was his father's boy. Even if Moria did run away, she would always be reminded of the love that she once had for Marcus. He was such a loving husband. What happened between them? Moria hung her head and let the tears come. If only she knew where they had gone wrong, but right now it seemed hopeless.

Moria did not hear Marcus' footsteps as he walked into the room. He took a few minutes to study his wife. She did not look happy anymore. Her face was always shadowed with sadness he never noticed before. Marcus knew that she was exhausted and that the new baby was taking its toll on her, but instinctively he knew that there was more to her sorrow. Earlier he had asked Moria to make sure the baby did not wake him in the night. He was going to the northern territories in the morning with a select handful of men. They were taking this journey looking for the king. King Cullen had been gone for many more months than anyone expected. Marcus needed his rest. Why couldn't Moria understand that? They had argued over the fact that he only thought about himself.

That thought kept Marcus awake for hours. He didn't think he even fell asleep. The first time the baby cried, he was about to get up, but Moria jumped out of bed sooner to take care of him. Marcus laid in bed feeling guilty, *she must be exhausted, I should go and help, but I can't feed the child, what am I supposed to do?* When the crying stopped, and Moria had not returned to bed, Marcus decided he should see if he could do anything to help.

Standing here in the doorway, he felt like he was stepping onto holy ground. The way that Moria studied her son, the tenderness of her caress as she followed the profile of his face made Marcus stand back. Now, He noticed the slight shaking of her shoulders and realized that she was crying.

"Moria?" he whispered. "Moria, is everything alright?"

Moria looked up with eyes that showed her hurt. Undoubtedly, she was surprised and embarrassed that Marcus saw her crying. "What are you doing up? Go back to bed. That's all you care about anyway."

Marcus wondered if Moria realized how much those words really hurt. "I haven't slept at all tonight. I couldn't stop thinking about you and what you said."

Moria looked at Marcus with eyes that flashed with anger. "Oh, well, I am so sorry to bother your sleep."

"Moria, what is wrong? I don't know why you are so angry," Marcus pleaded.

"I really don't want to talk about it. Go to bed, just leave me alone. You have a busy day tomorrow remember? Just leave me alone." Moria turned her back toward Marcus again and continued to rock Ronan.

Marcus watched silently for several minutes the ache in his heart was strong. All he wanted was to help her, why was she pushing him away so much? Quietly, he left the room and returned to his bed. Obviously, Moria was not ready to talk.

New Name

Cullen swam out from the safe haven. The food was running low, and he did not like the idea of running entirely out. Hunting would help him gather his thoughts. Cullen thought back to his early childhood. He had met King Oscar and Queen Aideen several times. They were very close friends of his father. All the memories that he had of them were good. They were kind and patient with people. King Oscar served his people with justice and mercy. As a young boy, Cullen didn't remember too much about the affairs of the kingdom, but he knew that Oscar and Aideen were concerned for the safety of their seven-year-old daughter. Their daughter's name was Sine. King Domnall and King Oscar had agreed upon an arranged marriage between Cullen and Sine. Cullen didn't mind, every time he was around Sine, they had a lot of fun. She was a couple years younger and full of life. She always looked for ways to enjoy life and make him laugh.

Cullen could distinctly remember the time they were enjoying a picnic at the lake with their parents She was probably just about seven years old, it was the last time he had seen her. Sine was wearing a light blue colored dress and skipping along the shore of the lake.

Turning to Cullen, she laughed and shouted, "Come on!" she teased with her eyes sparkling and challenging him to chase her.

Since Sine was not watching where she was going, she tripped over a turtle that had just crawled out of the water. Tumbling into the shallow water of the lake's edge. Cullen ran to help her out of the water but doubled over laughing at the sight. There she lay, her golden hair full of sand from the beach, her feet straight in the air and her brown eyes huge with surprise as to what just happened. Instead of being upset that Cullen was laughing, she started splashing Cullen, and her laugh was heard all the way across the lake. The memory made a smile play across his lips.

Cullen could still remember the time his father came into the room to talk with him. "Cullen," he said, "There has been a great tragedy."

Domnall's eyes clouded with tears as he told Cullen of the death of his beloved friends. There was a great division in Oscar's kingdom. Many people loved them, but some of his most trusted men wanted the throne for themselves and killed Oscar. Aideen died shortly after she witnessed the death of her husband. Sine was not found; many people were hoping that somehow, she had escaped unharmed. Domnall remembered talking with Oscar. He told him they were worried about Sine's safety and was considering putting her in a convent to keep her protected. Somehow, Cullen needed to explain to Keela that he knew her real name. She had been living and believing for so many years that her name was Keela. Would she listen to what he was about to tell her?

Keela couldn't help but feel like today was a special day. She woke very refreshed after an excellent sleep. She cheerfully hummed a song that was running through her head. Cullen had gone out early this morning to do some hunting. Keela had gone and picked some berries and ripe fruit for when he returned. With her back toward the water, she set the basket of fruit and a few flowers on the bench and did not notice Cullen had returned.

"Someone seems cheerful."

His voice had taken Keela by surprise, and she almost dropped the flowers she had in her hand. Keela glanced over her shoulder with an embarrassed smile. "You sure know how to make an entrance," she said. "You always surprise me when you show up like that." Keela turned around and noticed that Cullen did not seem his usual happy self.

Cullen placed the freshly hunted rabbits on the table, "We need to talk Keela." Fear gripped her heart.

"What's wrong?" The fear showed clearly in her eyes.

Cullen let out a sigh, "Why do you have to think something is wrong just because I want to talk?"

"Well, mostly because you look so serious like you have awful news or something."

Cullen's expression changed slightly. "Sorry, I have just been doing a lot of thinking, but it's not bad news, don't worry. Come, sit down," Cullen said as he patted on the open area on the bench where he was sitting.

Keela walked over and sat with Cullen, but she still could not get over the sense of dread that was threatening to pull her into a black hole of despair. Whatever happened to her cheerful mood that was just there a few minutes ago? *Come on Keela,* she thought to herself, *He said it was nothing to worry about. He is always asking you to trust him, right? Well, believe him!* Keela tried to read the expression in Cullen's eyes. Were they sad, angry or was it something else.

Cullen took in a deep breath and let out a heavy sigh. "Keela, please listen closely to what I am going to tell you. It's going to seem like an impossible story, but please hear me out and honestly think about it."

"Oh, Okay." Keela struggled to get the word out.

"Let me just tell this story from my memory. When I was a young boy, my parents had arranged a marriage for me."

Keela felt the tears in her eyes. *I knew this was too good to be true, figures, I fall in love with someone who I am not supposed to.* Keela was so lost in thought that she had stopped listening to Cullen.

"Keela, are you listening to me? Keela?"

Keela felt embarrassed. "I'm sorry," she said, "Your first sentence got me thinking about something."

Cullen sighed, "Keela, please listen carefully. I know you think this is bad news, but it really isn't."

Keela tried hard to focus on his words and give him her full attention.

"As I was saying," Cullen continued, "My father had arranged a marriage for me to marry his best friend's only daughter who was several years younger than me. Her name was Sine, I can still remember her. Her golden hair seemed to glow in the sunlight and beautiful brown eyes that were always dancing with laughter. The last time I saw her, she was about seven years old. I was nine years old, feeling like I needed to watch out for her as our parents talked. We went to the edge of the lake to look for frogs in the grasses ..."

Keela was having a hard time focusing on Cullen's story. She could feel her frustration rising in her heart. *Why is he telling me about a little girl he obviously loved when he was a young boy.*

"Cullen, why are you telling me all this?"

"Let me finish my story please Keela, I promise you will understand why I am telling you this story when I am finished. I know you will have a lot more questions." Cullen took in a deep breath before continuing, "As I said before, that was the last time I had seen her. It wasn't long after that when my father came to talk to me. He told me of an unfortunate story. His best friend and his wife were killed."

Keela involuntarily gasped. "Oh, that's so sad, I am sorry."

Cullen looked at her with a stern expression, his eyes that told Keela he wasn't done telling the story. "Oscar and Aideen were king and queen of the country of Esperanza. King Oscar had confided in my father, not only was my father aware that Oscar's kingdom was in turmoil, but he also knew that they were planning on protecting their daughter by having her raised in a convent. Oscar's most trusted warrior was the one who had betrayed the king. He had become selfish and wanted to run the kingdom on his own. King Oscar had enough loyal people that after they learned of the death of the king, a war broke out within in the kingdom. During the civil war, King Oscar's enemy, King Dorcha saw it as a perfect opportunity. They attacked the already war-torn country and completely wiped the kingdom out. Only a few peasants were left of the great kingdom. After the fighting ended, no one knew what had happened to Sine. People searched for her for years, but she was never found." Cullen turned and looked directly into her eyes. His look was serious yet gentle. "Keela, I know you are Sine." He hesitated a few minutes to let his words sink in.

Keela felt like the room was spinning. *What did he just tell me? How could that be true? Could I be a princess from the country of Esperanza? That can't be!*

"Keela."

Keela blinked several times like she was waking up from a dream. She looked at Cullen. "I can't believe that story," she stammered. Keela thought back to her years in the convent. They never told her who her parents were, and her past was always mysterious. Could it be true? Cullen's voice pulled her from her thoughts.

"Think about the times you spent in the dungeons. What were the questions they kept asking you? They knew your name was Sine remember? They even told you that you were a princess and wanted to know all kinds of information about your parent's kingdom and the kingdom that you were to marry into. I know it's a hard story to believe, but I am positive it is true. Not to mention, you look like a mirror image of your mother. Where was the Convent that you grew up in?" Cullen asked.

"In the valley of Lugar Sombrío," Keela responded.

Cullen was silent for a moment, "I would like to visit them and verify that you are indeed Sine. Would you give me permission to do that?"

Keela thought the idea sounded perfect. "Yes, the convent's abbess' name is Sara. Will you take me with you?"

Cullen thought about that for a moment. "I understand you want to come along, but the trip will be long, and it won't be easy."

Keela smiled, "I am sure I will be okay. Besides, I will be with you. Nothing can hurt me when you are with me." Cullen didn't reply to her comment. "Cullen, please let me go with you! I would love to see my sisters again."

"I am sorry, I can't let you come with me. It's only been a few weeks, and you're not strong enough to travel such a long distance. I will take you there when I think you're ready. Better yet, I will have the nuns travel to visit you when we are at Dia Richoet. I will leave at first light tomorrow."

Convent

Cullen traveled four days; now he was just a short distance from the convent. As he came to the end of the woods, he noticed the meadow that surrounded the convent. Sure, the pasture looked inviting and peaceful, but the grey walls of the convent looked foreboding and hard. It didn't look like an enjoyable or fun place to grow up; it seemed like a cold, lonely, unforgiving place. *So, this is where she grew up,* he thought, *doesn't look like much fun. No wonder why she seems so different from the young girl I remember.*

He approached the iron gate. Peering through the bars, it looked as if the convent was deserted. Cullen stood knocking and calling out for someone to open the gate. After excessive knocking, a young nun finally came to the gate.

"I am sorry, we are unaccustomed to visitors," she said in a timid voice. "How can I help you?"

Cullen looked at this young nun and imagined his precious Sine. "I need to speak with the Abbess Sara, please."

The young girl seemed nervous. "I'm sorry, Sara doesn't see visitors ..."

Just then an older woman began yelling from inside the convent, "Anna! Get away from that gate!"

Nervously, Anna looked over her shoulder, "Sorry, I must go." and turned to leave.

"Wait! I need to speak with Sara, please!"

Still, Anna hurried away. Cullen watched her turn the corner until she was out of his sight.

"Sara!" Cullen yelled, "I need to speak with you about Sine!" His voice was only met with silence. "Sara!" This time his voice rang with authority. "Sara! Open this gate and talk with me. This is King Cullen from Dia Richoet. I have traveled a great distance to meet with you; I will not leave until you agree to speak with me."

The young girl called Anna reappeared from the corner of the convent along with the older woman. As they got closer, the older woman spoke.

"No one visits with Sara," she began. "She is in solitude, praying and fasting." At this point, Cullen was getting angry.

"Well, then, I will wait until her fast is over. I did not travel this far for nothing."

Anna's eyes grew wide when she heard Cullen's response.

"Well, then," the older woman replied, "you better make yourself comfortable out there, a storm is coming, and these gates will not be opening anytime soon."

Cullen was surprised by the cold-heartedness of this woman, but he refused to let her send him away that easy. "Very well. I shall wait."

Storm clouds were on the horizon as the sun began to set. The cold winds began to stir and grow stronger as the evening grew late. Cullen had made camp just in front of the Convent gates as he said he would. Late into the night, the storm began to get very strong. From the dark convent courtyard, he heard someone walking his way. As he stood to see who was walking toward him, he recognized the older woman he had spoken with earlier.

"You are a very persistent man," The older woman said, "Who did you say you were?"

"My name is Cullen. I am King of Dia Richoet. I am betrothed to marry Sine. I need to speak with Sara about her." The older woman's eyes were a cold blue/grey color, and her tone of voice was as cold as her eyes.

"I have no idea who this Sine person is, and I am sure Sara would not know who she is either."

Cullen leveled her gaze. "That is for Sara to tell me, not you. I will not leave until I have spoken with Sara."

Cullen noticed an elderly woman in the convent doorway holding a lantern. "Open the gate and let him in," she said. Immediately, the older woman did as she was told.

Cullen was sitting in the chapel of the convent with Sara. The convent was very dimly lit, and the cold stone echoed every footstep regardless of how gently one walked.

"I am sorry for the way Dana treated you. She is very protective of me in my old age, and we are unaccustomed to visitors. I was unaware of your request to see me until Anna informed me that you were still waiting outside the gates."

"Thank you for meeting with me, Sara."

Sara sat on the bench opposite Cullen. Her expression told him that she was deep in thought. "I knew someday we would meet." Her expression was strangely sad. "I am sorry, but there isn't anything I can do. Sine is not here."

Cullen decided to ask a few more questions. "Did you know Sine?"

The older woman's eyes took on that far away expression. "Yes, I knew her for several years. She was the joy of my heart although I was never allowed to tell anyone. I was sworn to silence even though I felt like it would kill me. I loved her like my own daughter, but I needed to act like the tough Abbess. I was instructed to change her name and never allow anyone to know her true identity." A tear slowly made its way down Sara's cheek. "The day she left, I felt like I died inside."

Cullen felt like he had pried too much. "I am sorry Sara, I didn't realize ..."

Before Cullen could finish his sentence, Sara continued, "I have recently received word that she was killed by King Dorcha. My goal was to protect her from that man. I failed." Sara's head hung as if she was ashamed. Cullen noticed the gentle shaking of her shoulder and knew she was crying.

Cullen could keep silent no longer. "Sara, I have come to talk to you about Sine because she is not dead as you feared. I know where she is. She has been calling herself Keela for years, but I know she is really my betrothed Sine."

Sara blinked and said, "Can that really be true? Keela was indeed the name her father gave her when he told me to protect her. I obediently called her Keela. My heart just about broke when we heard of the death of our beloved King Oscar and Queen Aideen. Just knowing that my beloved Keela would never know her parents …"

Her voice trailed off as she became lost in thought. Again, Cullen could see fresh tears slowly rolling down the older woman's cheeks as she turned to look out the window. After several moments of silence, Sara began to speak again.

"I was instructed to take care of her only until she was eighteen years old. On her birthday, I was supposed to release her from the convent and give her the gift of independence."

Cullen gently placed his hand on Sara's. "Sara, I rescued Keela from King Dorcha's dungeon. She is safe with me now. I just needed to hear it from you that she really is Sine. I will bring her to visit with you soon when she is ready for a long trip."

Sara's expression changed from sadness to concern. "When she is ready for a long trip? Is something wrong with Sine? Is she sick or injured?"

Cullen wasn't sure he should tell Sara about the abuse Sine had to endure since she had left her convent. "She needs to rest before she travels, but she will be fine."

Silent tears slowly flowed down Sara's cheeks. "My precious Sine what happened to her? Why did I let her leave this place?"

"Sara, you are not responsible for what happened to her after she left the convent. You are a God-fearing woman and only did as you were asked."

Sara's looked directly at Cullen, her gaze challenging him to speak the truth. "My Lord, you didn't answer my question."

Cullen, who still wanted to spare the details replied, "Things were not easy for Sine. King Dorcha is a brutal man. The cost of her freedom was high, but now she is free, and I will protect her for all my days."

When Cullen had returned from his trip to the convent, he confirmed that the Abbess Sara did indeed prove that her real identity was Sine, princess of Esperanza, just as Cullen thought. Now it made a lot more sense that her parents just left her behind. It wasn't because she did something wrong like she believed all her life. It was because they loved her and wanted to keep her safe.

It still took her by surprise when Cullen would call her Sine. But each time he said her name, she felt happy. The name Sine did seem to fit her better. Cullen had once told her that Sine meant 'God is Merciful.' She thought about that quite a bit too. Indeed God was merciful to her. He had protected her many times in her life and now has led her to Cullen.

Sine sat surrounded by the flowers and berries. She took a deep breath in through the nose. The smells here were so sweet. The earthy tones mixed with the fragrances of the ripe fruit and the sweet spices of the flowers that grew all along the floor of the woodlands. Why was she so scared to leave this place? The idea of starting to travel again made her sick to her stomach. She had finally found peace sitting with Cullen. Just to sit with him and talk to him gave her such a feeling of security. Cullen had always shown that he loved her and that he would protect her no matter what. Why was she so afraid? Sine knew the bottom line was trust. She knew it upset him, but she didn't know how to have that kind of faith in him. Her anxious heart always took control of her feelings.

Cullen left the safe haven when Sine was asleep. She was about ready to travel. He needed to do a little hunting before they started on the trip. Cullen wanted to make sure they were both well fed, and he could dry some meat before it was time to head out. Sine was healing, and her strength was returning rapidly. Cullen was noticing Sine's attitude. Lately, it seemed like she was very anxious to leave this safe haven. Cullen thought about her lack of trust. Didn't she realize that every time that she worried about things, it hurt him? Cullen made sure that everything was taken care of every step of the way. Sure, she trusted him when Dorcha held her in the dungeon, she had no choice. Now that she is strong and healthy, she is more independent and not so willing to trust. Cullen knew very well that Sine was an independent-spirited person. All her life she needed to do things herself, now things were different. Cullen wanted to take care of all her needs because of his love for her.

Cullen finished hunting. He had killed, skinned and dried the meat of three large rabbits. Now they had enough food for their trip home. He just needed to talk with Sine about the trip. Sine was sitting among the flowers, in her favorite spot.

"Well, I have enough dried meat for our trip and then some. How are you feeling?"

Sine couldn't lie about how she was feeling. She needed to talk to Cullen honestly about it. "Well, I feel like I am strong enough now if that's what you meant. You know I don't want to travel."

Cullen sat on the grass next to her. "Yes, you have told me that you don't want to leave this place. I am well aware of that. Honestly, that is frustrating me."

"I know," Sine sighed, "I guess I need to talk to you about that and be honest with my feelings."

Cullen didn't say a word, but his expression told Sine that he wanted to hear what she had to say.

"I am sorry for upsetting you. I know you want me to trust you and I really do try to trust. I am not sure why I get so scared."

Cullen gave her hand a squeeze. "I know why you don't trust."

"You do?"

"Yes, you have been hurt before by many people."

"Perhaps, but you have only shown me kindness. I should not be struggling with trusting you, I am sorry."

Cullen took Sine in his arms and embraced her. He took in a deep breath, "Well, I won't tell you that it's okay. Honestly, it hurts each time I ask you if you trust me. I am waiting for the day where I will know the answer without question. Sine, I believe you will trust me fully one day. Hopefully, sooner than later." There was a comfortable silence between them for several minutes.

The Search

The men gathered in the morning to decide the best way to go looking for Cullen, they were watching the sky. It looked like a strong storm was brewing in the north.

"If we are planning on heading out, we better get going."

Marcus was looking at the men. Quinn, Fergus, Flannery, Kelly, Conall, Donnchad and Kier. They were some of the best fighters he knew. These men were not only the best fighters in the army they all loved the king. There was no question that they would lay down their lives for Cullen without any hesitation.

"Men, I know you all don't need to be reminded, but we don't know what we are going to find. If Cullen is not in the Northern territories, we will return home and start off in a different direction. I want each one of you to talk with the villagers. We need to know if they have seen Cullen, but we can't give them any cause for alarm. I don't know how long we will be away. Many of you have families here, if you would like to change your mind and stay here, please speak up now. We all know this journey could become very dangerous."

Marcus studied his men. Not one of his men even looked like they would change their minds, but he wanted to be sure. Marcus thought back to his own wife. *I wish I were leaving Moria happy. She wouldn't even say goodbye to me this morning.* Marcus dismissed the thought. He was the leader, and there was no choice but to go immediately.

Flannery spoke up, "If it pleases you, my lord, we are all ready to find the king. Not one of us is going to desert him now."

"Very well then, let us be on our way."

Marcus and his men had been traveling for seven days. All the villagers they spoke to in four different villages had the same story. They had not seen King Cullen even when people knew that King Cullen would have passed through the town four months prior, the story remained the same. Marcus knew that if King Cullen had come through these villages, he would have stopped to visit with the people. Cullen's love for his people was evident in all his actions. He never would pass by a village without stopping by to bless someone. Usually, he would have a meal with one of the most impoverished families in the town and later reward them for their kindness with a bountiful supply of food and cattle. Marcus met up with the rest of his men. They discussed what they had learned.

"I spoke with ten villagers this morning, and they all had the same story, no one had seen King Cullen," Kelly said.

"I met with several villagers also, but one older widow woman came up to me and said something I will not forget. She said she has known Cullen his whole life. Even as a young child, he loved the people. He would always stop and play with the kids, buy from the marketplace and share with those in need. He especially took time to visit those who were sick. She remembered one time that he stopped and met several young children who were very sick, but the parents could no longer afford the doctor's charges. They were sick with worry, and the parents only could sit and watch their beloved children get weaker and sicker. Cullen asked his father for help. King Domnall called for the doctors and told the doctors to do whatever they could to save the children. He would pay the doctors for the treatment. Now the children are all grown and strong. The two children grew into strong men and now served in the king's army. They have vowed to protect the king with their lives."

"We are the two brothers that she spoke of," said Kier. His brother Domnchad was looking down at the ground. "Our mother always reminded us of that story. Cullen knows we are the brothers and he almost wouldn't let us serve in his army. I am glad he changed his mind."

The other men mumbled in agreement. They all knew that Cullen was best known for his kind, tender heart for his people. Marcus couldn't agree more.

After much discussion, Marcus and his men decided to begin searching for King Cullen in the southern part of the kingdom. They had traveled a day until they came to the village of Neamhreireacht. Several villagers confirmed that King Cullen had passed this way. The only troubling thing was that nobody had seen him again for several months. Marcus watched as dawn broke. The sky was painted with beautiful pink shades that turned to golden streams of light as the sun came up over the hillside. His night watch was over; now it was time to put the smoldering fire out and wake the other men.

"Come on men; it's time to keep moving."

As the men stirred, Marcus heard a rustling sound in the forest just a short distance from where they had kept camp. The men reached for their swords and began quietly heading toward the sound. As they got closer, Marcus noticed that the animal that was rusting the bushes was a horse. Why would there be a horse in the forest? As they got closer, Marcus recognized the markings and knew it was Hunter, Cullen's favorite riding companion. Yes, Hunter was the only horse that Marcus ever saw with the black mane and tail along with the black socks around his feet like that.

"Hunter?"

The other men immediately realized that it was Cullen's horse, also. Marcus could tell by expressions on their faces. Concern and worry marked the eyes of every man.

"Why would Hunter be here by himself?" Conall said, "He doesn't have any saddle or bridle, perhaps Cullen is near."

"Let's spread out, men. I don't think Hunter would venture far from Cullen." Marcus kept his fear to himself. He had never known Cullen to let Hunter wander. Did something happen to Cullen?

The thought of something happening to his king made his stomach tighten. "There is eight of us total. I want everyone to stay in a pair and search in different directions. Kier and Dunnchad, you two head south. Conall and Kelly you two head east. Flannery and Quinn head toward the west and Fergus, and I will go north. As you go, do an extensive search heading in different directions. In other words, Kier and Dunnchad you are heading south, but sweep toward the east and west. You should meet up with Conall and Kelly in the east and Flannery and Quinn in the west. That way we will cover all the ground and still keep in touch with each other."

The men had searched all day. Nobody had seen anything that was even the slightest bit of encouragement. Their voices were strained from calling throughout the day. Marcus had seen a large lake with an open clearing. *This would make an excellent place for an encampment* Marcus thought to himself. He decided to have his men all meet there as dusk fell and make camp. Surely tomorrow they would search again. Now, they needed their rest.

Cullen's Men

Cullen slipped into the cold water located within the cave. He swam the familiar waters and surfaced just behind the waterfall. Cullen had always made sure he surfaced in that location because he could see the surroundings before he was seen. This evening was no different. As he surfaced, he immediately noticed a campfire burning on the beach. Even though it was dusk, Cullen swam carefully underwater toward the shore where the marsh grasses would give him additional cover.

In the stillness of the night, Cullen could hear a group of men and their conversation. As he concentrated on being as still as possible, a large, venomous water snake swam by. Cullen shivered inwardly, he did not like snakes, that was for sure, but as long as he was still, the snake would not bother him. The snake swam toward the shore where the men were setting up camp. Cullen observed the men as the poisonous water snake approached them. *This should stir things up a little. Maybe I will be able to get a look at one of the men's faces if they get up to kill the snake,* he thought.

Sure enough, just as Cullen was hoping, the snake drew attention from the men. As the men sat around the fire, the man facing the shore stood to his feet.

"There's a snake right behind you." That same man started walking toward the snake with his sword. He was a small man of stature with bright red hair and a heavy limp as he walked.

Cullen watched the men on the beach *Is that Flannery?* As the man lumbered toward the snake. Cullen squinted to see the man's face. *That must be Flannery, I wish I could see his face to be sure.* He thought to himself. Just then, Cullen heard a familiar voice.

"Thank you, perhaps it wasn't such a good idea to camp next to this lake. Fergus, it is your turn to stay on guard through the night. Keep an extra eye out for any more snakes." Cullen knew that voice anywhere. It was Marcus, his best friend. Although Cullen couldn't make out the rest of the men, he knew that they were his men, looking for him.

As Cullen swam to shore, he began talking so he would not startle his men.

"Marcus! I wondered how long it would take you and the men to find me."

Marcus immediately spun around. "Cullen!" He stood and embraced him as a brother.

Cullen acknowledged the other men, "Men, thank you for looking for me."

"My lord, you sure made it difficult. How did you find us? Why were you in the lake?" Kelly said.

Marcus chuckled, "Well, I was not trying to be found. Instead, I was in hiding. I will explain more soon. Right now, I would like to speak with Marcus alone."

As Cullen and Marcus walked a short distance, Cullen began to explain the situation to Marcus. "Marcus, I have found her."

"My lord?" Marcus seemed confused by Cullen's excitement.

"Remember when I told you that I could hear a woman calling for me at night? She was in pain and scared."

Suddenly realizing what Cullen was talking about Marcus responded. "Yes, I remember that, how did you find her?"

"I did as you suggested. I continued to travel until the voice became clear. That's why I have been gone so long." Marcus looked confused.

"What do you mean? How did you get her free and where is now? When were you planning on coming home?"

Cullen took a deep breath. "It's a long story Marcus, one I will tell you more about at a later date. As to when I was planning on coming home? Well, I was hoping to leave in a day or so. I needed to wait until Sine was ready to travel, but now that you're here, I would rather travel with the company."

When Cullen returned to the cave, Sine could tell he wanted to head to his castle. "Get a good night's sleep. In the morning we travel." The thought of traveling both excited her and scared her.

"How long is the journey?"

"Two, maybe three day's journey." Cullen looked at her. "Sine, just to let you know, we will not be traveling alone. Eight of my finest warriors will be traveling with us." Sine's mind was spinning.

"What? How?"

Cullen went on to explain, "My men selected a group to search for me. I have been gone from my kingdom for over four months. Well, during their search, they found this lake. Right now, they have made camp on the far side of the lake. I have just spoken with them."

As Sine tried to sleep, she realized the amount of responsibility that Cullen set aside to find her. How could she ever repay him? She drifted off into a fitful night's sleep knowing that all too soon it would be morning.

The Journey Begins

Early the next morning, Cullen helped Sine swim out of the safe haven that they had called home for the past three weeks. The cold water was refreshing, and the feeling of Cullen's hand in hers gave her a sense of peace. She was not as scared of the water anymore. Cullen had clearly shown her that he was there to help her, not to harm her. She could trust him entirely now. As they surfaced behind the waterfall, Cullen kept his hands around her waist to prevent her from sinking back down, under the water. He held her as they swam toward the shore.

"You can stand now," he said,

Willingly, she obeyed and stood to her feet. As they walked the remaining distance to the shore, she observed the soldiers on the beach. All of them were standing ready to help. Their love for their king was evident on all their faces.

Cullen was introducing her to the men.

"Sine, this is my best friend and companion, Marcus."

Marcus had a cheerful smile, and his brown eyes seemed as though they were smiling. Although he had short stature, he looked tough. Sine could just imagine that he would not be pleasant to deal with when he was angry.

Marcus felt as if all he could do was stare. Sine was amazingly beautiful. He didn't see any sign that she was mistreated. Her long blond hair smooth from the water. Since it was still very wet, it had a shimmering appearance. Marcus thought that her hair in that light resembled liquid gold cascading down her back. She was young, but she must be brave. Cullen had indeed found a beauty among women.

Next, Cullen introduced her to two men who were apparently twins.

"This is Fergus and Conall," Cullen said with a chuckle. "These brothers have helped me win arguments with other kings."

The two men smiled. "It was our honor, my lord," Conall said.

Sine wondered what the little joke was that she apparently was unaware of.

"This is Kelly, my fearless warrior."

Sine was surprised that this man seemed young. She guessed that he was close to her age. His eyes were full of life. His smile was not forced.

"This is Flannery, a very selfless warrior. He would and has put others safety before his own. In fact, that's why he has this limp. Every time I see him walk, I am reminded of the time he saved my life from a wild horse when I was just a boy."

"My lord, I am humbled. I was only doing my job."

Sine watched this man; he had evidently been injured more than once. His stature was the shortest of all the men. He had fiery red hair, and his limp was very pronounced. Yet, he was humble.

As Sine turned around, she was surprised to see an older gentleman standing next to Cullen.

"Sine, this is Quinn he is a wise man. It would do you good to get to know him a little."

His silver hair was carefully groomed, and despite his age, he still looked like a very healthy warrior.

"My pleasure to meet you," she said.

"Likewise."

Although Sine sensed that he did not trust her or perhaps he didn't like her, she wasn't sure, but she knew one thing, she would have to earn his friendship.

Finally, Cullen brought Sine over to meet the last two men.

"This is Donchad and Kier; they are brothers. They feel they owe me their lives. At first, I didn't even want them to join my army because I didn't want them to serve just as a way for them to pay me back, but they have shown to be the most loyal men I know."

Sine looked at these two men. They were of average height, and they seemed embarrassed to be spoken of in such a way. She noticed a seriousness about them, and they did not smile. Both men had curly brown hair and green eyes.

The journey was nothing like Sine had expected. She had never been treated with such respect in her whole life. Kelly, the young soldier, was funny and full of life just like she had thought he was. His small talk helped pass the time. Leading the pack of men, Marcus and Cullen were mounted on their own horses and talked almost the entire time they traveled. Sine's heart was torn. *Is this how it's going to be? It's almost as if he forgot I was even here,* she thought to herself. Just then Cullen turned toward her.

"How are you feeling? Do you need a break?"

Sine lied and said, "No, I am fine." Suddenly, Sine remembered that he could hear her thoughts and she felt embarrassed. "Well, not totally fine."

Cullen looked over his shoulder at her and smiled. She could feel that he was not upset with her.

The two loyal brothers were walking on either side of her horse. One of them had given her his horse while the other brother's horse was laden with the supplies. Because of his limp, Flannery always rode a horse and led the horse that was used to carry supplies. The twins kept to themselves, and the older soldier was at the tail end of the caravan.

As dusk began to fall, Cullen and Marcus were looking for a safe place to camp for the evening. When they had settled on a location, Marcus started to give the men orders to set up camp. Marcus was glad for the amount they had traveled in one day. If Sine was up to it, they could be home in a few days. He was thinking about Moria, was she aware he was going to be gone this long? How was she handling

Ronan on her own? He let his thoughts take the forefront of his mind as he prepared to make camp.

Cullen dismounted Hunter and walked over to Sine's horse. He helped her dismount. "How do you feel after riding a horse all day?"

Sine massaged her sore legs. "Well, I am very sore I feel my muscles where I didn't know I had muscles before." She laughed.

Cullen knew that she would be sore but hearing her laugh at her own stiffness made him smile. *There's that determination I knew was there,* he thought to himself.

Sine continued. "Right now, I am starving, after a meal and a good night's sleep, I think I will be able to do that again." She winced, her face still holding that confident smile.

"Well, I better get busy finding you a good meal then." He turned toward Marcus and said, "Marcus, let's form a small hunting party while the other men prepare the camp."

Sine was already awake before the dawn. She stared at the sky and watched the colors slowly spread across the sky. The deep purples turned to reds and pink splashes across the clouds until the pinks faded into a golden glow. *That has to be the most beautiful sunrise I have ever seen,* she thought to herself.

Not as beautiful as you, my dear, I am surprised you're already awake.

Sine sat up quickly and saw Cullen back to her, spreading the fire to cool the ashes.

"Good morning," she said.

"Morning. I didn't mean to startle you," Cullen said with a smile.

"It's fine; I just need to get used to the fact that you know my thoughts."

"I may be able to hear your thoughts, but you can hear mine as well if you listen."

As Sine tried to stand, the pain in her body took her by surprise. Her legs just didn't want to work. Cullen came to her side quickly and steadied her on her feet.

"Let me guess, those muscles you didn't know you had are screaming at you now?"

Sine chuckled, "You could say that, but the muscles that I did know I had are screaming too!"

Cullen's eyes were tender, "Do you want to rest here another day or two until you feel better?"

Sine wanted to say yes, to beg him to let her stay, but she also knew how badly he wanted to get home. "It's only a few days, right? I'll do my best to make it," she said trying to keep her smile convincing.

"You're amazing, Sine. Honestly, it would be okay with me if you wanted to wait another day."

"Please don't hold back on my account, if I can't keep going on, I'll tell you."

Sine couldn't get over the amount of pain she was in. She didn't realize how difficult it was to ride a horse for so many hours. The determination was setting in her mind. *After everything he has done for me, I will do my best to make it to his castle. Then, I will rest.*

Again, this trip the twins walked on either side of her horse and Kelly was busy talking to her and telling her jokes. *Is he is telling me jokes and silly things to make me laugh just so I would forget about the pain?* She thought. This time she listened to Cullen's thoughts.

Yes, sweetheart, it is obvious to all the men here that you are not comfortable. Kelly likes to be light-hearted, he knows it helps people who are nervous or in pain. Cullen let his horse slow down, so he was walking the same pace with Sine.

"How are you doing?"

"I don't really want to answer that," she replied.

Cullen looked concerned. "Are you sure you don't want to stop and rest? We have already made good progress. We are far enough into my territory; I am sure we are safe. We will be coming close to a village if you would like, we can stay there."

"No, it's okay, I am determined to make it to the castle."

"Very well, please don't hesitate to tell me if you change your mind. I really don't like seeing you in pain. You know full well that I would do anything I can to help you right?"

"Of course, I know. Thank you."

The sun was still high in the sky, and Sine was beginning to wonder if she really was not going to make it all the way to the castle. As they came over the crest of a hill, she could see the castle in the far distance. They were almost there! As they came close to a village, many people came out to greet them.

Sine heard the voice of one little girl over the crowd of people.

"Mama, the king has returned! The Mighty Men are riding with him! Mama, who is that woman that rides along with the king's men?"

Cullen must have heard the young girl's comments also because he slowed his horse down to walk astride her.

"Please, come and ride with me in the front. That way everyone will know you are with me, not my men."

Sine spurred her horse slightly faster. Marcus, understanding what was happening, slowed his horse to make room for her in the front.

As Sine rode next to Cullen, she was amazed the people absolutely adored their king. Children danced in the streets. Men and women alike tossed bright colored blankets or their own coats on the road ahead of them lining the road.

"Long live the king!"

Their cries filled the air. Men and woman bowed low before the king as he rode down the street. Cullen was acknowledging different people by name. It was evident that he was familiar with many of the villagers, their livelihood, their families and their struggles. Sine glanced at Cullen, *Yes, Cullen deserved their praises. He deserves all praise. He is a mighty and powerful king, yet, he is loving, and cares for all the people in his Kingdom with great compassion.*

Cullen caught a glance of Sine. She was looking a little bewildered, but the expression on her face told him that she was not concerned, just surprised. He studied her for a moment. Her long flowing hair was gorgeous in the evening's light. She gave pleasant smiles to all his people as they walked by even if they did not acknowledge her. *Yes,* Cullen thought, *she is going to make a perfect bride. She already treats my people with love and respect.*

Sine was interested in one thing, not only did Cullen know them by name and he took the time to talk with them. Sine noticed that she didn't see a single beggar in their midst. While Cullen was talking to one elderly man, Sine walked her horse over to Quinn.

"I don't see any beggars in the villages," she said.

"You're absolutely right," Quinn replied.

"Why?" Quinn smiled. "About nine months ago, Cullen became disturbed by the thought that there may be one person in his kingdom that did not have a home, a place to get in out of the cold. It happened right before our first snow of the year. Since that time, he has housed all the beggars in the kingdom and helped them all find work or work to make a trade of some kind."

Sine turned to look at Cullen. He was still talking with the elderly man.

"You see that man he's talking to now?" Quinn continued. "He was about to die. We found him, barely alive, curled up on the frozen ground and very starved. Cullen took such compassion on that man; he paid the doctor of the village to nurse him back to health. Since then we have learned that his name is Cameron and he used to have a busy shop as a goldsmith. His wife fell ill, Cameron sold his shop and home to pay for doctors hoping to save his wife, but she passed away. When Cullen heard of his story, he had a new shop built for Cameron. With a lodge above the shop."

So, Cullen is compassionate and kind to all people, not just me, she thought.

"That's what makes him the greatest king beside his father."

Sine had not heard anything about Cullen's father.

"Please tell me about his father."

Quinn thought fondly about King Domnall.

"King Domnall is Cullen's father. He is slow to get angry. However, when his enemies rise against him, his wrath is great. He will command his mighty armies to protect his own people. Most of his enemies run and hide if they know they have provoked his wrath. To his people, he is a gracious king, kind and compassionate. He rules his kingdoms with great wisdom and justice." Quinn paused as he remembered something.

"So, he's alive? How can Cullen be a king if his father is still alive?" Sine asked.

"His domain covers many kingdoms. He has appointed different leaders over each kingdom to oversee them. He picked his son, Cullen to rule as king over Dia Riochet for a while."

Cullen had stopped talking with the elderly man and came to Quinn and Sine. "I have been speaking with Cameron. He has requested that we stay at his house, have dinner with him and spend the night. We will finish our trip to Dia Richoet after we eat."

Sine let out a sigh of relief, and Cullen chuckled quietly.

"I take it that sounds like a good idea to you, Sine."

She felt the heat rise in her face and knew that her embarrassment was visible to both Quinn and Cullen.

"Yes, my lord, it sounds wonderful to me."

Cullen turned to his friend Marcus, "I know you are eager to get home, but Sine really does need a rest."

"Yes, sir," Marcus responded, but in his mind, he was thinking about Moria.

Alone

This morning Moria's mood was much more cheerful. Perhaps her attitude was better because she was alone. She wasn't sure what made her upset whenever Marcus was around. Many times, she would become grumpy as soon as Marcus said 'hello.' Perhaps her mood was changing simply because Ronan was beginning to sleep more at night. Sure, she was still exhausted, she barely got any sleep last night, but it was the first time that the baby slept for four hours without waking. Moria woke up a few times during those four hours. She was afraid that something was wrong with Ronan, but each time she checked in on him, he was peacefully sleeping.

Marcus had been gone now for more than two weeks. She thought back to their last conversation. *Well, I got what I asked for.* she thought to herself, *I told him to leave me alone, but I didn't know he would be gone this long. I hope everything is alright. What if something did happen to him? Why did he go without saying goodbye to me?* A knock on the door interrupted her anxious thoughts. *I wonder who that could be,* she wondered as she headed for the door.

Moria was surprised to see a young woman standing by the door. The young woman's face was flushed, and she was breathing hard as she leaned against the house.

"What is the matter?" Moria asked.

"Is your name ..." the young woman was gasping for air. "Moria?"

"Yes, are you okay?" Moria was beginning to get concerned.

"Please, I need your help." Again, the woman was trying to catch her breath. "My father is injured." Moria glanced around her house. She had not been filling the job of a doctor since Ronan was born.

"Please!" the woman said again. Her breaths returning to a slower pace. "I know you are a doctor." Moria didn't need to give it a second thought.

"Let me get a few things. Come in." Moria carefully wrapped Ronan in cloths and fastened him to her back. *I wish I had more supplies, I don't even know what condition this man is in or what happened to him,* she thought as she carried the few supplies she might need to help this man.

Moria wasn't sure if it was the fact that she hadn't gotten much exercise since Ronan was born, or if it was because Ronan was strapped to her back, but she had a tough time keeping up with the young woman. After several minutes, they came to a field.

"Daddy! I'm coming" the woman yelled, and Moria could hear the emotion in her voice. "Hold on Daddy! The doctor is coming!"

Suddenly the young woman began to run. Moria could not run with Ronan on her back so she followed as quickly as she could. She could see the young woman kneel next to a man lying on the ground. As Moria approached, she could tell that this man's injuries were terrible.

"What happened?" she asked as she looked at the man's wounds. He had severe cuts in many different places.

"I don't know!" the woman said, "He was plowing the field with the cattle, and I came out to bring him a drink. This is how I found him."

Now the woman buried her head in her hands and began to cry. Moria tried her best to help this man but was helpless to save him. Too much time had passed since his injury, and she didn't have the right supplies. Moria did what she could, but it was not enough. After she consoled the woman the best, she could. She helped her get the man's body back to their house. As Moria turned to walk back to her home, the sobs of the young woman filled her ears, and confusion filled her thoughts.

Moria couldn't stop wondering if she had done absolutely everything for that man. She had never lost a patient before, and this was devastating. Suddenly she remembered her younger brother. She remembered holding his head in her lap as she watched his life slip away. It was too much for her to bear.

As she entered her house, she called out, "Marcus?" The silence of the house reminded her that he was traveling, and she didn't know when he would return; she never felt so alone in her life. How she just wanted to be held by his strong arms and to hear his comforting voice. Marcus always knew just the right thing to say. *Oh Marcus,* she moaned, *I'm sorry. Why have I pushed you away?* Numbly she took care of Ronan and laid him on his bed. Finally, the tears came. Moria wept for the man that died, for the young woman who was alone, but mostly for her regrets. She felt as if she had failed as a doctor and as a wife.

Home

The dinner at Cameron's house refreshed Sine, and she was again ready to travel. After they were outside of the village, Sine set her sights toward Dia Richoet. The closer they got, Sine noticed the beauty of the countryside that surrounded the castle was breathtaking. From where they were Sine saw that they were on top of very steep cliffs that dropped straight to the ocean below. The smell of salt was pungent in the air and when the wind blew, she could feel the mist from the crashing waves. There were only a few trees that would hinder the view of the castle, and most of the trees were bent from the constant blowing of the ocean winds. A large cove was between where they were standing and the castle. From that view, Sine could see that the majestic castle stood high on a hill. The foundation for the castle walls were parts of the cliff, and other areas of the wall were built into the cliff. The meadow that was on the opposite side of the castle was full of wildflowers with herds of white sheep that dotted the countryside. Just below the castle in the valley was another village. Sine could not see much of that town, but she imagined it must be one of the busiest in his kingdom.

Cullen had been watching Sine's expression. Sine turned toward Cullen and in the excited voice she shouted

"Come on!" Commanding her horse into a full gallop.

Cullen gave a lighthearted laugh, wasn't that the same thing she said to him right before she tripped over that turtle? Cullen accepted the challenge and commanded Hunter into a full gallop,

"Let's show her how fast you can run, boy," he whispered into the horse's ear.

Hunter seemed to understand what Cullen said and took off in a full gallop until he had caught up with Sine. Sine was laughing so hard that Cullen thought she would fall off her horse.

"Oh!" she was gasping for air. "Oh! You should have seen the look on your face!"

Cullen chuckled, "You want to know what was going through my mind when you said that?" Cullen said with a grin.

Sine dismounted her horse and came to stand near Hunter,

"You're a fast boy!" She exclaimed as she caressed the horse's face. With eyes that were still dancing with laughter, she looked up at Cullen. "Yeah, what was going through your mind?"

Now, it was Cullen's turn to laugh. "Well, I just remembered what you were like when you were seven years old," he smiled, "I remember the last time I had seen you like it was yesterday. We were playing by the lake, and you started skipping. You turned toward me and shouted, 'Come on!' exactly like you just did. Perhaps the reason I had a strange look on my face was what happened next. When you had turned toward me, you were not watching where you were going, and you tripped over a turtle. Next thing you knew, you were laying in the water with your feet straight in the air." The thought of it made Cullen laugh.

Sine didn't see it as funny as Cullen did. "You mean you just laughed at me? Didn't you help me?"

Cullen had a difficult time controlling his laughter. "Well, once I saw you were not hurt, we both laughed. Sine, don't you get it? That same fun-loving girl that I knew is still there. Although I must admit, I was afraid you might trip over a turtle again." Again, Cullen began laughing.

Sine could not help it; the laughter began to bubble up within her as well. "Oh, it feels good to laugh, Cullen. The problem is, I forgot how sore I was until just now." Sine gave a pouty face which made Cullen smile.

"Do you want to rest for a few hours? We are almost there, but this is a good spot to stop and have something to eat."

Just then, Marcus and his men were approaching.

"Marcus, we are stopping here for a few hours,"

Cullen shouted toward his men, "We are going to stop here for a few hours and have something to eat."

Marcus was clearly confused. He dismounted from his horse and walked up to Cullen.

"My lord, we are almost home, why stop here? In just an hour we can be in the castle enjoying dinner."

"I know, but I think Sine needs a break."

Marcus looked at Sine then back at Cullen. "But, she just took off in a full gallop! Unless that's why you want to give her a break." Marcus looked as if he just realized what he said. "Of course, sir, we will take a break here for a few hours."

Sine felt the heat rise in face but was grateful for the chance to get off the horse for a while. After a short break and the rest of their food rations, Cullen approached Sine.

"How are you feeling?"

"I'm okay." She said feeling guilty that she was the reason the men did not make it home for dinner. "I think some of your men might still be hungry, it looked like the food ran out before they all were full."

"If you are feeling well enough, I would like to finish our trip home. It would be a lot more comfortable for you to sleep in a soft bed than spend another night sleeping on the hard ground, and my men are anxious to see their families."

"Oh, yes! Off course! I am sure I can make it to the castle now. That break helped, but we won't get there before nightfall. It's already getting dark."

"Your right, but we can travel a good distance even with the dimming light, once night falls, we will be close enough to the castle I am not worried about traveling at night."

"Very well," Sine said. "I'll be ready to go when you say so."

Cullen Smiled. "Thank you, Sine. I know my men will appreciate it." Turning back towards his men, he said "Men, time to go home. I know dusk is upon us, but if we move now, we can be within the castle walls just after dark."

Immediately, the men sprang into action, Marcus stood and put dirt on the fire to extinguish the flames, while the other men began putting supplies onto the horses.

Mounting his horse, Marcus said "Okay men, time to go home." Sine turned to Cullen who was already seated on his horse,

"Is there a reason Marcus seems so anxious to go home?"

"A few months ago, his wife Moria, gave birth to a baby boy. I don't think Marcus has been home much since. He misses his family."

Sine was quiet. *I am so inconsiderate,* she thought to herself, *all I have been thinking about was my problems. These men gave up so much to help us, and here I am sitting complaining that I'm too tired to finish the journey.*

Cullen's voice interrupted her thoughts. "Sine, it's not inconsiderate if you didn't know."

Looking at Cullen's gentle expression she said, "Perhaps, but that's how I feel."

As they rode, Marcus changed the formation of the men. This time, Cullen and Sine rode side by side in the center with the men riding in front alongside and behind them. They did not talk but were alert.

"Why are they riding like this?" she asked Cullen.

"Because we are riding at night. They are protecting us. With darkness, comes danger that you cannot see until it's upon you. They are riding like this to make sure nothing gets close to either of us. They are silent, listening for any danger."

After riding in silence for an hour, they were now approaching the castle. The light from within the castle cast a gentle glow on the street, a welcoming sight to Sine.

"Cullen, it's so pretty!" She whispered.

"Yes, she has a beauty to it at night, doesn't she?" Cullen seemed to be looking at the castle for the first time. "I never noticed how pretty the castle looks in the evening."

Suddenly there was a shout from near the castle walls. "The king has returned! Open the gates! The king has returned!"

Immediately the gates open before them; people came from their homes to greet the king just like they did in the village. The celebration and dancing were even more enthusiastic here within the castle walls. After the grand procession into the castle, Cullen helped Sine dismount.

"The stable workers will tend to your horse. Come with me; I want to show you around. The castle was so grand. Cullen introduced her to a few of the maids who would be able to help her if she had any questions. *It's been so long since I've slept in a soft bed, I think I forgot what it feels like.* Sine thought to herself, as they headed to her sleeping quarters.

Sine, I know you're exhausted, get some rest. You can explore the castle more tomorrow."

"Thank you, Cullen."

"Glad to have you home with me." Cullen turned and headed for the door. "Sleep well."

"Good night."

Marcus / Moria
reconciliation

Marcus wondered how Moria was. Did she even miss him? Sure, the baby was taking a lot of Moria's time and energy, but what else was the problem? Moria had once suggested that Marcus should find another woman. What did she mean by that? Did Moria think he was unfaithful? Or did she just not love him anymore. Marcus tried to think. Had he done or said anything recently that would make Moria feel like she was not needed or loved? Marcus tried to think about any conversations where he might have said something that hurt her. The truth was, they had barely spoken since the baby was born. Perhaps that was the problem. He would make sure to talk to her and give her some time to have fun together again like they did before the baby was born, and Marcus began traveling looking for the king.

Marcus had planned the perfect surprise for Moria. It took a little work, but he was finally able to convince Nancy, their longtime neighbor, and friend, to watch the baby for a few hours. Now, the hard part would be convincing Moria to leave the baby.

Marcus stepped into his small house and looked around. Moria did not know that he had returned, and he wanted to surprise her. After looking in the kitchen, Marcus headed toward the back of the house to find Moria. As he approached the bedroom, he could hear her sweet voice as she was quietly singing to the baby. He stopped just outside the doorway, listening to the gentle melody for just a minute. Marcus realized that he had not heard her sing in a very long time. He remembered when they first were married; she often sang as she made dinner for them. Her voice was like an angel. Marcus had entirely taken her singing for granted. Now, the song stopped him in his tracks. She did sound like an angel.

Quietly he walked into the room, afraid to disrupt the moment. Moria stood back to the doorway. Marcus studied her. She looked tired, her shoulders slumped slightly forward, and her hair was not put up into the neat bun that she regularly wore. Her eyes looked swollen like she had been crying very hard or she had not slept in a long while. Marcus quietly cleared his throat. Startled, Moria looked at Marcus. A flash of anger was in her eyes. "You know you shouldn't startle me like that!" Moria whispered motioning to the baby. "I finally got him to sleep, don't wake him up!" Marcus stood silently in the doorway as he watched Moria put Ronan into the bed. Once Moria was confident that the baby would stay sleeping, she turned and walked toward Marcus.

Marcus sat down in his favorite comfortable chair. "Come here, Moria."

Moria came and stood next to his chair, "Yes."

Her tone was icy, but Marcus pretended he didn't notice. Nothing was going to ruin his plans, not today.

Marcus could feel the laughter in his eyes. He smiled and said, "No, I mean to come here, sit with me."

Moria was surprised by the smile in his eyes, she hesitated. "Trust me; you don't want me to sit on your lap. I think I'll break it," she said with a chuckle.

"That's impossible; you won't break me. Please, sit with me like old times." Moria sat gingerly on Marcus' lap. Marcus let out a groan that was obviously exaggerated, and they both began laughing so hard the tears were flowing down their cheeks. Marcus had a faraway look in his eyes.

"Remember the hours we would sit together like this and dream of our future?"

"Yes, if only we could go back in time. Those were the good old days." Moria said.

"Why should we have to go back to those days? Why can't we still live them now?" Marcus was studying her, he wanted to know the answer to that question, and he wanted to be sure that she was as truthful as possible.

Moria thought for a moment. "I don't know," she said, "Perhaps it is because now we have responsibilities? You know, the baby keeps me so busy I feel like I don't even exist anymore, and you are so busy helping Cullen, you're not here very often."

Marcus thought *Well, I can't complain I wanted her to be honest.* Instead, he cleared his throat and said. "I'm sorry Moria, I never wanted you to feel like I wasn't here for you."

"I sure was feeling that way. I felt so trapped here in this house. Ronan took so much of my time and strength, and you were always busy. Soon I felt like you were using me as a servant, not a wife." Moria looked at Marcus; she could tell that the words that she had just spoken hurt deeply. "Marcus, I am sorry, I shouldn't have said any of that."

Marcus swallowed hard; His throat was thick with emotion. "It's okay; I was hoping you would be honest with me, I just didn't realize how badly you were feeling."

"Marcus, there's more." Marcus braced himself at what she was about to say. Moria lowered her head "I lost a patient yesterday." Just saying the words brought the tears on again. "I'm sorry," she sobbed, "I've failed as your wife, and now I've failed as a doctor."

Marcus couldn't believe what she was saying. "Sweetheart, you didn't fail as my wife. I'm sure you didn't fail as a doctor either. You always do your best. You have never lost a patient; it must have been horrible. I'm sorry I wasn't here for you." As he held her, the tears slowed and finally stopped.

Marcus figured now was as good a time as any to announce his plans. He held Moria at arm's length so he could look into her eyes. "I have made plans to take you somewhere special, just you and me. Nancy promised to take care of the baby for a few hours. I think we need to spend some time together." Moria looked as if she was about to protest the idea but soon changed her mind.

"Are you sure Nancy will be ok with the baby?"

"I'm sure she will be fine, she has five children of her own. I know she knows how to take care of a baby, and her oldest daughter is old enough to help a little." Marcus could tell that she was still hesitating. "We could leave now. The baby is asleep, which will give us a little more time."

Suddenly the idea sounded terrific to Moria. The chance to spend a few hours with just Marcus sounded heavenly. "Really?! This isn't a joke or something right? I mean you wouldn't do that to me, would you?"

Marcus laughed out loud at her comment, and the sound of it made her smile. "You know, I haven't heard you laugh like that in a very long time," Moria said.

"Well then, it sounds like it's a plan. Let's get the things that Ronan will need, and we can be on our way. Nancy's daughter will stay at our house until the baby wakes up. Then she will take him back to her house where her mother will watch him."

Moria kept reminding herself that she wasn't dreaming. Did Marcus realize how frustrated she had become? As they rode on horseback, Moria noticed that he had already packed food and a blanket to sit on. "Where are we going?"

Marcus smiled. "Just wait a few minutes, you'll soon see."

She rode alongside him in silence for a while. *If I only have a few hours of peace, I don't want to spend it riding the whole way* she thought.

"Marcus, seriously," she began to get frustrated, "I don't want to …" Her voice caught in her throat. As they rounded the bend, she saw the most beautiful field filled with all kinds of wildflowers and a huge shade tree. "Marcus!" Her voice was barely a whisper.

Marcus looked at her. "I take it you approve?" His eyes were teasing her with laughter, but she did not care.

"Approve?! I never saw this place before. It's beautiful."

"Well, that's one of the benefits of my job. I see a lot of beauty here in the kingdom. When I saw this place, the first thing I thought of was sharing it with you. I couldn't wait to bring you here."

Moria's eyes still took in the scene in front of her. Marcus was enjoying the expression on her face. "When did you find this place?" she asked.

"I found it during our first search for King Cullen. I would have brought you here sooner if I could have, but my first and foremost responsibility is for the king, you know that."

"Yes, I know, but I must admit, as selfish as it sounds, I was getting very jealous of the time you spent for Cullen. It's been so hard taking care of the baby by myself."

Marcus spread out the blanket on the ground, under the broad shade tree, surrounded by delicate wildflowers.

As Moria sat down, she said, "Did I see you bring some food? I am starving!"

"Yes, darling, I brought lunch for you. but I'm starving for time with you, not food."

Moria's gentle laugh filled the air. "Oh, you're such a romantic!" She said.

"You think I am kidding? Food nourishes the body; love nourishes the spirit."

The hours flew by as they reminisced about the times they first met. Marcus promised to help around the house with Ronan, starting with watching the baby tonight and into the morning so Moria could sleep soundly through the entire night.

Moria woke to feel refreshed. She didn't wake up at all during the night, not even when Marcus left the room to take care of the baby. As she stood, put her robe on, she smelled eggs cooking on the stove and freshly brewed coffee.

"Ah, sleeping beauty has woken up!" Marcus smiled at her as she entered the room.

"Wow, I can't believe how good it feels to sleep the night through without waking up."

"Good, I'm glad to hear you slept. I worked very hard to make sure nothing woke you up."

"Breakfast smells delicious! You cooked all this for me?!"

"Of course! It's my pleasure. I realized that you have never tasted my cooking. Normally it's over an open fire, but the stove did nicely for me."

"Thank you, honey. I appreciate all that you have done. How did you sleep?"

Marcus chuckled. "Sleep? I was supposed to sleep?!" His laughter filled the kitchen. "I guess I slept as good as you have the last several months. Now I understand why you are so tired. I spent the night sleeping on the floor here in the kitchen with the baby on my chest."

Moria was surprised by his response. "What! Why?"

"Because I didn't want you waking up every time I got out of bed."

"Honey, you didn't need to do that. You should have stayed in bed."

"Well, you slept soundly, right?"

"Yes, I did."

Marcus smiled, but his eyes showed that he was serious. "Then a 'thank you' is more than enough."

Slightly embarrassed, Moria said, "Thank you."

Marcus smiled "Now, enjoy this breakfast I prepared for you. I need to go to the castle and see if Cullen has any requests for me. I'll be back as soon as I can."

Marcus spotted Cullen in the grand hall.

"My lord," Cullen waved him into the room.

"Marcus, I trust you are well."

"Yes sir, thank you for asking."

Cullen had a thoughtful look on his face, "Marcus, I have noticed that you were distracted during our trip home. Please tell me, how are you and Moria doing? I know that after Ronan was born, the two of you were not on good speaking terms."

"Well, things are much better right now. I took some time to listen to Moria and helped her with the baby. I need to make sure she doesn't feel taken advantage of."

"Marcus, I know you very well, you never would take advantage of Moria. Why on earth would she think that?"

"Those were not her exact words, but it was apparent that is how she felt. It was more the fact that I never helped with the baby. I was sleeping soundly through the night while she was staying up at night taking care of the baby. She was exhausted. Then when she needed the most support, I was not home."

Cullen thought for a few moments. "Well then, I don't have anything that needs to be done right away, go spend a week with your family. It sounds to me that you have been traveling a little too much lately."

"Thank you, my lord," Marcus said as he bowed low before Cullen. Marcus turned to head back to his house. He looked forward to spending time with his family for a while.

Throne Room

Two months had passed since they got home. *This is precisely what I was afraid would happen,* Sine grumbled to herself, *I have not seen Cullen since the day we got here.* Sine stayed in her room most days; her appetite practically gone. If she got hungry, she often requested her dinner be brought to her, because she just didn't feel comfortable eating in the dining hall.

That morning, Sine stood, gazing out her window. *I feel so lonely,* she thought, *it's almost as if I am still in a dungeon. Yeah, sure it's a comfortable room with a soft, warm bed and the food is so amazingly delicious, I just feel so alone. I suppose I should go out and try to find people, but I hate trying to talk with complete strangers.*

Taking a deep breath, Sine decided to make the best of her situation. She would bathe, put her hair up, and get dressed in the prettiest dress that Cullen gave her. *Didn't Cullen say I could explore the castle? He wouldn't mind if I walked around a bit. I wonder why he hasn't come talk with me.*

Sine anxiously walked through the castle hallways. As she came to a large room, she heard many mumbling voices. A large curtain hung in the doorway, one on either side of the entrance. Sine touched the curtain, gently feeling the satiny texture of the material. It was beautiful. An excellent craftsman undoubtedly made it. No doubt it was made with the most elegant linens. The colors were vibrant blues, purples, and crimsons and the craftsman had worked beautiful angels into the curtain. Taking a closer look, Sine could see that the curtain had been torn. The other half of the curtain still hung on the other side of the doorway. *How could a curtain so thick be torn? It's huge! The floor to the ceiling had to be at least 15 feet. Who could rip a thick embroidered cloth so far?*

Standing next to the curtain, she became partially hidden from the room. Timidly, she peeked into the room and immediately realized it was the throne room. Sine's eyes widened at the appearance of the room. This place was the most majestic room she had ever seen! It had marble pillars and floor. The curtains that lay along the sides of the windows were made of the silkiest velvet. The color was deep purple and almost had a fluid appearance. It was simply breathtaking. *I have never seen a color like that! It looks like it's moving!* She thought.

The people in the room were standing shoulder to shoulder. There was barely any room to move! Sine noticed that people from all different ages and different trades were standing together not regarding the people they stood next to. The wealthy were not offended to stand next to a sick widow, and the beggar children had no problem standing next to the farmer. That's when Sine noticed Marcus as he walked around the room. He was busy talking with the people. After speaking with several people, he would turn and speak with the king.

I just want to run in there and talk with Cullen like we did before. Sine felt the tears sting her eyes but refused to allow them to fall. *I can't barge into the throne room! I need to be asked or invited. I could get into so much trouble, I have heard of people getting put to death for entering without permission. What am I doing?*

Sine observed Cullen, he sat on his throne, watching the people. Marcus would come to him with the piece of parchment and speak to Cullen. After a short discussion, Marcus would again return to the person he had spoken with and give them a new white piece of parchment. The person would turn and walk out of the room. As soon as they walked out of the room, more people would step into the room. *So many people! How can he possibly help each one?* She wondered. *How foolish of me to wonder why he hasn't come to visit me. I better just go back to my room before he sees me, but it's so lonely there.*

Immediately, Cullen turned and looked straight into Sine's eyes. Sine was shocked that Cullen knew she stood in the doorway. *Oh, I forgot he knows my thoughts, but with all that commotion in the room, how did he even hear me?* All the people in the throne room including Marcus fell silent as they noticed King Cullen's attention shift toward the doorway. Cullen had known that she was getting lonely and wondered why she had not come to visit him sooner. It was clear to Cullen that Sine was afraid to be in the throne room.

Sine knew that she could no longer hide behind the curtain, cautiously she stepped out and began walking toward Cullen. Cullen studied Sine as she walked into the room. He couldn't tell what it was, but he knew something troubled her. Her shoulders were low and, as she walked, she did not let her eyes leave the floor. Her gait was slow and labored, almost as if something had been tied to her ankles, weighing her down. Now, she had walked across the entire throne room and stood before him, trembling from head to toe. Sine still did not look up. Her eyes fixed on the floor at his feet.

"Sine, what is the matter? Why are you trembling?"

Sine still did not look up. Instead, she dropped to her knees. "My lord, forgive me, I know I am not to come into your presence here in the throne room without you requesting me."

Cullen stood to his feet and crossed the short distance between them. "Sine, look at me." Gently, Cullen helped Sine to her feet.

Slowly, Sine lifted her face, but she still didn't dare look into his eyes.

"Sine, I said look at me."

Sine finally was able to look into Cullen's eyes, what she saw was pure love. His eyes had no anger or hardness to them at all. What she saw was only gentleness and concern.

"I am sorry," her voice was barely a whisper, "I am very selfish."

"How are you selfish?" Again, his eyes were gentle and full of love, his voice showed no anger or harshness.

"I am selfish just because I haven't seen you for so long. I thought if only I could see you again, maybe the loneliness would go away. I know I am not supposed to come to you unless you ask, forgive me for being so bold. Now that I am here, I see how busy you are. I am sorry for not believing you could be that busy." Sine could feel her frustrations mounting. The more she tried to explain herself the sillier she sounded. "Oh, I am just rambling now!" She moaned.

Cullen took her in his arms and held her tightly against his chest. She felt the peace begin to fill her senses as he continued to embrace her.

"Sine, there is one thing you need to understand. You are never a bother to me. In fact, I was wondering why you had not come to see me sooner." Cullen held her by her shoulders at arm's length so that he could look deep into her eyes. "Sine, I don't want you lonely. Honestly, I want you here with me! Didn't you understand that?" He motioned toward his throne. Sine looked in the direction that he was motioning toward and noticed a second seat sitting empty to the left of his throne. "That seat is yours. I've been yearning for the day when you would come and join me. I want you to come boldly into the throne room. I want you to sit by my side as I attend to the needs of my people and rule over any injustices. Please," Cullen took her by the hand and walked her toward his throne. "Sit by my side and talk with me."

Marcus came before Cullen and handed him a large parchment. "My lord, I have these requests from your people. Some of them are asking for your help, and others are looking for guidance."

It only took a few moments for Cullen to look over the concerns that Marcus brought before him. He took out a pen, and with a fresh white parchment, he wrote his answers to the concerns. Cullen looked up at Marcus.

"Here, give these to the people. If they follow the directions, they will find what they need."

Marcus nodded and bowed before the king. "Yes, my lord." Marcus returned to the people to give them the answers to the concerns they had shared.

"I don't understand," Sine whispered, "Why only give them directions? What if they need food or shelter?"

Cullen looked at her and smiled. "You see, in my message I give directions to take care of their need. If they need food, I give specific written directions to go to the king's banquet hall and dine with me. However, if they are too proud to read the directions, they will go hungry. If they are looking for a job, I give instructions as to where to receive a job. I know every master craftsman in the kingdom, they are instructed to give jobs to those who come and ask for work stating that the king sent them. Again, if people are too proud to read my instruction, or not willing to work, my advice will be useless. Those who choose to read and obey what I wrote will find their need met."

Sine was lost in thought. *What wisdom! I never thought that some people would just want the king to take care of all their needs while they sat and did nothing. I guess that's what I've been doing, too!* Sine began to feel guilty.

"Cullen, your wisdom is very great. I must appear foolish to you."

Cullen waited. He wasn't sure what she was going to say next, but if he always told her she was alright, she wouldn't grow and change.

"Forgive me," Sine took a deep breath and willed herself to continue, "I have been very selfish. I mean, all I did for these past several months have been sitting around, waiting for you to visit me. I've locked myself in my room as if I was a prisoner and felt sorry for myself."

Cullen still did not say a word. He wanted to let Sine tell him all her thoughts without interruption.

Sine noticed the silence, it felt very awkward at first, but she glanced in his direction and saw that he did not look angry. "What should I be doing with myself? I don't want just to sit here and expect people to take care of me."

"I am glad you asked." The smile in Cullen's eyes matched the bright smile on his face. "There are things that only you can do. Do you believe that?"

Sine shook her head slowly, "Not really, I am not important, and I don't have any great abilities. I don't have any idea ..."

Cullen interrupted her, "Sine, here's what I want you to do. It's something that only you can do."

Sine blinked back her tears; she knew that Cullen always looks for the positive in her.

Cullen began talking again, "Since you have experienced my great love for you, I want you to show that same great love to others."

Immediately Sine wanted to object. *Oh no! That's an impossible task! I don't even like talking with people, how am I supposed to show them, love? Doesn't he know I can't do that?*

Cullen was still speaking; the sound of his voice shook her from her thoughts. "I know you may not think it's possible for you to do this, but as you begin to meet and befriend people in the villages, you will see your love for them will grow."

"So, you want me to go into the villages?"

"Yes, what I want you to do is begin to make friends with the women of the villages. When they tell you their needs and problems, tell them about me so I can help them. I know many of my people in the villages don't know that if they just come to me, I'll take care of them and their families."

Sine thought about that for a moment. "Why don't you want me to befriend the women here in the castle?"

"Well, there is nothing wrong with befriending the women here in the castle courtyards, but they already know about me and how much I love my people. They know that I will protect and provide for them at all costs."

Winter is past

The day was a warm spring day. Sine was reclining on her couch when Cullen entered the room. He went to the window and motioned Sine to come. Cullen stood cradling Sine in his arms as they both overlooked the landscape beyond the village. Flowers filled the meadows, and the fruit trees were blossoming with fragrant buds. It seemed to call them to walk the fields that are turning green in the spring sunshine.

"See! The winter is past; the rains are over and gone." Cullen said. "Come, my darling; my beautiful one, come with me."

Hunter was already dressed in his saddle and a second horse was tied next to Hunter ready for a passenger.

Sine turned to Cullen, "I take it you were already planning on going out for a ride?" She felt her eyes dancing as she lovingly teased Cullen.

"Yes, I had been planning this trip for several weeks now. I have lunch all packed and the perfect place to show you."

As they traveled north, Cullen took them on a path that ran alongside the ocean.

"Oh, Cullen the views are breathtaking!" Sine said as she wrapped her cloak a little tighter around her shoulders. The sun was warm, but the breeze coming off the ocean was cold.

Cullen seemed to take note that she was chilly and turned the horses inland. "I think it should be a little warmer if we got away from that breeze."

Sine loved the views of the ocean. "It's fine really; I love watching the waves crash on the rocks. I don't mind the coolness."

"Well, that may be true, but you will like the views inland too." After riding for a few minutes, the horses came to a crest in a large hill. The crashing waves were still within earshot, but they were sheltered from the wind with the bushes and flowering vines that dotted the landscape.

"Let's stop here." Cullen dismounted his horse and came to help Sine from her horse.

Once the horses were secure, Cullen turned to Sine and took her in his arms.

"There's something I need to tell you," Cullen began, "I am with you for only a short time longer."

Sine felt the breath catch in her throat as she felt the panic rise in her heart. "What do you mean? Are you leaving me? Where are you going?"

"You can't now follow me where I'm going. You will come later."

Cullen's smile was genuine, and the expression in his eyes gave Sine a sense of peace even though she was very puzzled at his words. He looked slightly past Sine's head and with a faraway look in his eyes and smiled. The smile brightened his whole face. He looked back into Sine's eyes his eyes were brimming with emotion.

"Oh, Sine, don't let your heart be troubled, trust me. There is more than enough room in my Father's home. I am going to prepare a place for you! When everything is ready, I will come and get you, so that you will always be with me where I am."

Relief flooded Sine's heart. "You will come back for me?"

"Of course!" Cullen said with a lighthearted laugh. "I rescued you with my life; I will never desert you. You are mine, altogether lovely. I am going home to my father's house to prepare the wedding feast! As I said, when it's all ready, I will come and get you."

When they returned to the castle, Cullen brought her to the Great Room. There, with several people around, he sat down and wrote out his marriage proposal to Sine. This caused a great celebration among the people. As she observed Cullen hang his declaration to the wall, she couldn't help but feel overwhelmed. *I can't believe I am going to marry Cullen! How is this possible?* Sine's spirit soared. It felt like it was just yesterday she was locked in a jail cell, not even knowing her real name and thinking she would never be loved because she wasn't worth it.

Be Alert

Cullen knew that his time was fast approaching when he would leave to go to his father, King Domnall. Today he wanted to speak with Marcus alone. As Marcus came into the throne room, Cullen knew now was the best time to talk with him.

"Marcus, please come with me."

Marcus silently followed as Cullen walked out of the throne room. "My lord, is something upsetting you?" Marcus asked.

Cullen turned and smiled. "No, I just need to talk with you alone."

Soon they were in the royal stable and Cullen was mounting Hunter and Marcus was mounting the horse that stood saddled and ready for him. They went for a short ride to the cliffs overlooking the ocean.

Cullen stopped Hunter and dismounted. "Here we can talk without interruption." After they had tended to the needs of the horses, Cullen allowed Hunter to graze on the sweet, tender spring grasses. "Marcus," Cullen began, "I know you are already aware that I plan on going back to my father, King Domnall."

Marcus tried to hide his surprise. "Yes, my lord, is that why you brought me all the way out here?"

Cullen looked at his friend. "Marcus, you know me better than that. I want to speak to you at length about what I want you to do while I am gone."

Marcus suddenly realized the seriousness of the conversation.

Cullen continued, "I know that once King Dorcha has learned that I am away, he will begin to plan an attack. I will be gone for quite some time as I meet with my father."

Marcus interrupted Cullen, "My lord, I will not allow King Dorcha to attack. My men and I will remain loyal to you, and fight for you even if you are not present with us."

Cullen gave Marcus a friendly slap on the shoulder. "I am not questioning your loyalty to me Marcus!" he said with a light-hearted laugh. "I simply want to give you my instruction."

Marcus was embarrassed that Cullen would question his loyalty. "Yes, my lord," he mumbled.

"Please be alert. I know the ways of King Dorcha. He is very deceitful. His purpose is to steal, kill and destroy my people and the kingdom. I believe he will try to have his people settle in Dia Richoet. They will try to ruin my domain by moving in the villages and convincing my people that I have forgotten them or that I am not a good King."

"Cullen," Marcus could feel his frustration mounting, "Please give me the word, and I will destroy anyone who attempts to settle in Dia Richoet."

"No Marcus, I don't want you to show violence to the villagers. Instead, I want you to welcome them in Dia Richoet." Marcus could not believe his ears.

"Cullen! Why would you want to allow them to settle? They are our enemies! If you know they are going to try to destroy your kingdom, why would you welcome them?"

Cullen's expression was thoughtful. "Marcus do you think all the people that reside in Chrioch Olc under King Dorcha are happy there? Think about the stories we have heard of how brutal he is to his people. Think about Moria and her family. Don't forget Kelly and his family. How many other warriors have come to us begging for protection from King Dorcha either for themselves or their families? This may be the only chance these people may have to get freedom."

Marcus was frustrated. "Cullen, you are a gracious King and one who cares about all people, I admire you for that, but are you sure you want to risk losing your people or your kingdom to give a few the taste of freedom?"

"If I lose the loyalty of some of the people, they were never really loyal to me. They just enjoyed the benefits of my reign". Cullen looked out over the ocean. "Marcus, you are a warrior by nature, so this is difficult for you to understand. I want you to focus your skills and teach all my faithful subjects how to bear arms."

"My lord, won't that cause your people to become afraid?"

Cullen let out a deep sigh. "Some may become frightened, and some may lose their loyalty to me, your job will be difficult at times. I don't want any of my people to be frightened, they need to be trained for war and ready to fight, but most importantly they need to be confident that they will not lose the war." Cullen studied his friend. "Marcus, I know I am giving you a great task with a lot of responsibility. However, I know you are more than capable."

Marcus could feel the weight of the responsibility that Cullen was placing on him. "My lord, what should I say to your people if …"

Cullen interrupted Marcus's thoughts, "Let them know I will be back as soon as I can, never to lose hope, have strength and courage! Marcus, you are going to lead these people. Give it everything you have, heart and soul. Make sure you carry out all that I have commanded you, every bit of it. Remember, strength! Courage! Don't be timid; don't get discouraged. Since my father's house is not close, I will not be able to send you messages quickly, just know that when my father tells me it is time to return, I will come. I will return with my father's army. We will defeat this enemy once and for all!"

Marcus looked at his friend. "Cullen, does Sine know any of this?"

Cullen's eyes took on a faraway look. "No, not yet. She is aware that I am leaving, but I need to talk to her about being ready for war."

"How do you think she will handle your news?"

"I am sure she will be scared, she seems to be afraid of just about everything lately. With your training and patience, I know you can train her to become a confident, mighty warrior. I will speak with her before I leave."

Goodbye

The stone wall surrounding the window was cold and damp. Sine shuddered with the chill as she leaned against the wall. The storm felt like the perfect match to Sine's mood. She gazed out the window as the wind blew the heavy rain against the glass. All of nature was affected by the strong winds and fierce rainfall. Trees were bending in submission to the winds, and the grass in the meadow was being tossed about like waves on the sea. She watched a few villagers as they braved the storm to check on their livestock. *Those unfortunate animals,* she thought, *they cannot find shelter from the rainstorm.* Almost immediately, she remembered her days living outside when she stayed in Mormhuir Cathair. How many nights she tried to find protection from the weather. The first snowfall was still vivid in her mind. *I really wondered if I would make it through that winter. What would have happened to me if Cullen did not rescue me from King Dorcha? Surely, I would have been killed by now.* As she stood by the window, her thoughts turned to what Cullen had said to her the last time they were together. *Why is he leaving me? Why can't I just go with him?* She felt the tears sting her eyes as she willed them not to come. *Come on Sine; he's still here, don't be sad now!*

Cullen stood in the doorway for a moment watching Sine. She stood leaning up against the wall focused on something outside. Her long golden hair fell to her waist in gentle flowing waves. There were a few short strands that stubbornly curled around in a semi-circle on the side of her face. He couldn't see the expression in her eyes, but he could sense that she was deep in thought. As he stepped into the room, Sine turned around to face him. Although it was a fleeting expression, Cullen noticed how quickly Sine hid the sorrow that he first saw in her eyes.

"Well, hello!" Sine said, "I was just thinking about you."

That comment surprised Cullen. Now, looking into her eyes, he saw no sorrow, just joy, and happiness. "If you were just thinking about me, why did you look so sad?"

Sine immediately turned and looked out the window again. Cullen walked up behind her and wrapped his arms around her in a firm embrace.

"Cullen, I don't want you to leave." Sine's voice was choked with emotion. "I remembered what my life was like before you found me. What's going to happen to me while you're gone?"

Cullen rested his chin on Sine's shoulder and gazed out the window. "Sine, you always worry too much. Nothing is going to happen to you while I am away. Marcus is going to make sure of that." Cullen straightened and gently turned Sine around to face him. "Besides, I have a lot of work for you to do while I am away. You will be busy, and your mind will not have time to dwell on these concerns that are not real."

Sine looked up at Cullen. "You have work for me to do? You mean befriending the villagers? I'm still not sure how to do that …"

Cullen interrupted her thoughts, "I still want you to go to the villagers, but I have another job for you."

Hopeful that perhaps Cullen would change his mind about the villagers, she asked, "What is it?"

Cullen was trying to choose his words carefully. He knew Sine would disagree with him if he said she would make a great warrior. "I want you working with Marcus."

Sine breathed a sigh of relief. *Well, that doesn't sound too bad, I like Marcus.* She thought. Realizing Cullen was still talking, she turned her attention back to him just in time to hear him say.

"I instructed him to teach you, and all my loyal subjects to learn to bear arms."

Sine felt her eyes grow wide with fear. "What are you talking about?! Who would I be fighting? Why would you leave me if you know there will be a fight? You just said nothing would happen to me!"

Cullen sat down on the bench and motioned Sine to come and sit beside him. "Sine, I don't want you to become afraid. I just want you to be prepared. I have asked Marcus to teach you the bow, but I also want you to learn how to handle a sword."

Sine felt like her world was turning upside down.

"Sine," Cullen continued, "Please understand I know you are surprised by my request but know that I would never ask you to do something you cannot handle."

Sine tried to calm her mind enough to think about everything that Cullen was saying.

"Sine, look at me," Cullen's voice was gentle, he needed her to understand that this was for her own good, not to put fear in her heart.

As Sine turned to look at Cullen, he noticed that the look of fear was subsiding."I remember when you were seven, you were so full of life. Even though you were little, you took on problems with determination. You were very confident in yourself. I know that same girl is still there, sure, you have gone through difficult situations, and if you wanted to, you could use your past as an excuse to hide. Please, show me that confident girl I know is still there."

Sine smiled a timid smile. "Cullen, that was a long time ago."

Cullen felt defeated. He sat next to Sine with his arm draped across her shoulders. They sat in silence for several minutes.

"I'll do my best to make you proud," Sine whispered.

Cullen felt his heart leap and relief flooded his mind when he heard her words. "Thank you. I know you will learn quickly."

Cullen was still concerned about the underlying issue that seemed to take away all of Sine's joy. "You know, you still haven't told me the real issue." Cullen turned to see Sine better. "I am still waiting to hear you tell me why you don't want me to leave, I know it's not just because you will miss me. I can tell that deep down you're scared."

Sine's smile disappeared. She immediately realized how much they needed to talk. The more that she thought about her feelings, she felt so childish and foolish. How would she ever be able to express her feelings?

"I don't know if I can really explain what is scaring me."

"Why?" Cullen studied her beautiful brown eyes; they were definitely troubled.

Sine became shy under Cullen's gaze. "Because I feel stupid."

That response completely caught Cullen by surprise. "Stupid?! Your feelings are not stupid. Please, tell me what is bothering you."

Sine bit her lip. "I am scared that you will realize that you don't want me around." Immediately she felt like she was accusing him. She stood and took a few steps away from him. "I mean, you're a King of a large kingdom. I have nothing to offer. I don't know the first thing about your people. You will probably become busy and just forget about me." Again, she realized how she was sounding. "Oh, forget it! This is frustrating me! It's not your fault. I can't even figure out what is really bothering me." Sine felt the heat in her face. Cullen had not said a word, and now she knew that she had hurt him with her words. "Sorry," she whispered. "I told you, it was stupid."

Cullen was having a hard time hiding the hurt that those words gave him. *How could I possibly forget her? Does she remember what I did to free her from her enemies?* Countless times he told her and showed her that his love for her was real. He loved her for who she is not for what she has to offer. Honestly, he thought they had already gone over this.

"Sine, what do I have to do to prove I love you?" As he began talking, he noticed that his voice was strained with emotion. "Remember all the things I have already done for you? Why would you even think I would get to busy for you?"

Sine was standing a few feet from Cullen, her back still toward him. Cullen wanted to hold her again, but this time he wanted her to come to him. "Sine, please come here."

Sine glanced over her shoulder and saw Cullen standing with his hands held out waiting to embrace her. "I can't," she whispered hoarsely. Everything within her wanted to run and hide. *How can he still offer me his love when I continuously doubt him?* Sine could hear Cullen's voice, strained with emotion.

"Sine, one day you will not doubt my love for you. You didn't choose me, remember? I chose you. I came to your rescue not because you forced me to, but because I wanted to."

Sine still did not turn around to face him. After waiting several minutes, Cullen silently stepped out of the room and prepared for his journey. At sunrise, he would set off on his voyage to his father's house.

After several minutes the silence was too much for her, she turned around ready to run into his embrace and beg for his forgiveness, but he was gone. Sine sat on the bench near the wall where he was sitting just moments before and wept. She cried till she had no more tears to shed. There were too many emotions welling up in her heart. She did not want dinner, she just went to bed exhausted from weeping.

Sine was awakened to the voice of Cullen quietly calling her name as he knocked on the door. "But I'm in my nightgown. —Do you expect me to get dressed?" She didn't jump out of bed but remained for a minute. Again, Cullen knocked on the door and tried the latch. Sine jumped out of bed, brushed her hair, and put on fragrant oil. She unlocked the lock and opened the door, but he was gone. Cullen had gotten tired of waiting and left. Sine felt like she died inside *Not again!* She thought, running out looking for him, but he was nowhere to be found. She called for him, but there was no answer.

The morning sun shone brightly in her window. Sine was tempted to pull the blankets up and cover her head. Suddenly, she remembered why she had such a bad night's sleep. She had tossed and turned all night wondering why Cullen seemed so urgent to talk to her last night. The memory was all too clear. Immediately, Sine jumped out of bed and got dressed. The first thing she was going to do was find Cullen and apologize for not getting up to talk with him.

Sine came around the corner of the throne room, it was empty. She went to the Great Hall and saw that it was empty also. *Where is everyone?* She wondered. Sine heard voices and cheers from an open window. Running to the window, she looked outside, a vast throng surrounded Cullen. Hunter, loaded with bundles, stood beside Cullen as he said goodbye to the people. With her heart pounding, Sine rushed through the Great Hall, and past the courtyard to get to the place where she last saw Cullen. The crowd was so thick; they stood shoulder to shoulder. She could not easily pass. Determined to reach Cullen, she pressed through the crowd. As she got close, she heard Cullen talking with Marcus.

"Marcus, please take care of Sine until I return. You and Moria should stay here in the castle where all your needs are met."

Sine could not keep silent any longer. "Cullen!" she shouted as she pressed past the last few people that were separating her from where Cullen stood. "Where are you going? Why are you leaving me? I'm sorry I didn't ..."

Cullen silenced her words with a kiss. Then taking her hands in his, he looked deep into her eyes that were brimming with emotion.

Sine began to protest, "Cullen, please don't leave. I know you wanted to talk with me last night, what were you going to tell me?"

"Sine, after our last conversation, I was hoping to spend time with you before I left. I did not want to leave until I had the chance to talk with you again."

Sine could not stop the tears that spilled from her eyes. Cullen gently wiped the tears from her cheek. Cullen glanced towards Marcus, "He will see to your needs while I am gone. Just remember, after things are prepared, I will come back for you to make you my bride." His eyes were bright, and his expression told Sine that he was sincere.

"I will wait for you, my love," Sine said with her voice strained with emotion. *How long will he be gone?* she wondered but knew better than to ask that question.

Cullen knew what she was thinking, "I will come back when things are ready. I do not know the day or hour. I must wait until my father tells me things are ready. Rest assured I will come back as soon as I can. You will be in my heart and mind every day. I love you, Sine."

Cullen's eyes lingered on hers for just a moment longer, then he released her hand and turned to mount Hunter. The crowds cheered and shouted, their goodbye's and fair wishes to Cullen. Sine watched as the tears freely fell from her eyes. Most of the villagers had returned to their daily duties. Children laughed and played in the streets as if they didn't know that their king was gone.

Marcus watched Sine in the distance. This indeed was not easy for her. How long was she going to stand there staring?

Marcus approached Sine. "Why do you stand here staring where you last saw him?" Marcus' words startled Sine. "Cullen will come back in the same way you have seen him leave."

"I wish I could still talk with him." Immediately Sine felt the heat rise in her face. "Oh, I didn't mean to say that out loud." She said shyly.

Marcus smiled. "Sine, you're a very confusing woman."

Sine turned to look at Marcus and could tell he was teasing her by the smile in his eyes. "Oh really!" Sine said as she put her hands on her hips. "And why is that?" She said with an exaggerated pouty expression on her face.

Marcus needed to hold back his laughter. He liked the way she took teasing so well. "Sine, why don't you just talk to Cullen yourself?"

Sine just stared at Marcus with a completely blank expression. All teasing was gone.

"Sine, the two of you can communicate just as you did when you were in the dungeon."

Sine let out a gasp.

Marcus continued, "You do realize you're the only one who can talk with him now, right?"

The excitement began to fill Sine's heart. "I hadn't thought of that!" She whispered half to herself.

New Beginnings

Marcus had been given orders by Cullen to stay in the Castle and tend to the daily needs of the kingdom while he was away. Moria knew that was a great honor for Marcus, but a challenge for her. Moria looked around her house. She would miss the quiet, humble cottage that she had called home for the last few years

This spring she had found it nearly impossible to plant the vegetable with Ronan acting up as often as she had, but she had managed to get the vegetable garden planted nonetheless. Now that it was well into the summer the fruit of her labor was about to be spoiled. She strolled through the garden admiring the herbs and all the fruits the different vegetables were producing. She wouldn't get to enjoy the vegetables during harvest now that they were moving to the castle. Perhaps her neighbor could benefit from the bounty the plants would produce. It would be a shame to let them just rot on the vine. Moria turned and walked to the front of her house. There, the roses were in full bloom, and the fragrances were rich as they filled the air. *Well,* she thought, *I don't need to let these go to waste. I'll pick a huge bouquet and bring them with me to the castle.*

Inside, Moria looked around the cottage. She reminisced about the many hours she spent with Marcus as he so lovingly built their home. The fireplace was her favorite. Marcus would bring in all different sizes and shaped rocks and carefully fit each piece as if it was a puzzle. When the mortar was still wet, he would carefully place smaller river bed pebbles of all types of colors and shapes to add a beautiful design. Moria ran her fingers across the smooth stones. *Marcus, you made this like a piece of art,* she thought. The living room and kitchen was one large open area with the fireplace in the center. It was open on both sides. Moria used the hearth for cooking and heating the small cottage during the winter months. In the summer, she tried to cook outdoors as much as possible, or the temperature in the house would become unbearable.

The sleeping quarters were located to the left of the living area. They were small, and Moria did not like spending too much time there. Her room was reasonably large but only had one window. It always seemed dark and dreary. During the winter months, the stone walls emanated with coolness. The only window faced the north, so no direct sunlight ever shone through. Ronan's room was even more dreary. Since Marcus needed to build that room in the winter quickly, it was much smaller and had no windows at all. Marcus always said that as Ronan grew, he would make a new room that was sufficient for Ronan.

There was no question that Moria would miss this place, but she was determined to make the best of this new start at the castle. Moria wasn't sure how long they would be at the castle, but she decided it would be better to pack extra things instead of making many trips back home. As Moria packed their belongings in the crates, She watched as Ronan crawled around the on the floor. *Perhaps it would be best if we did not have an open fireplace with Ronan crawling around as much as he does,* she thought, *he's so active now that he is crawling. Always curious and getting into things; I think I will have my hands full once he begins to walk.* With the items she carefully packed all stacked in the corner of the room for Marcus to bring to the castle, she turned toward Ronan.

Ronan, playing with the neighbor's cat, protested when Moria picked him up. "Come on Ronan," Moria said. Ronan still continued to wriggle to try to free himself from her grasp. He extended his arms toward the cat on the floor as if he was asking the cat to help him get down. Moria smiled, Nancy's cat was a sweet companion for Ronan.

She was very patient with the baby, and if he got a little too rough, the cat just walked away. She never scratched Ronan although several times Moria thought she should have.

As she left her house, she made her way to Nancy's house. Nancy was a long-time neighbor who had helped her many times over the years. She had a large family and was always worried about feeding all the growing children. Moria knew just who should benefit from her vegetable garden.

Nancy's house was a humble place. Moria often thought it was too small for Nancy, her husband, and their five children. Nancy never acted jealous of the families in the village with larger houses. "It's not the size of the house that matters." She would say, "it's the amount of love in the house that matters." Nancy's family was rich in love, laughter and encouragement would practically spill from those small walls.

As Moria approached the door, Nancy came to the door to greet them. Nancy watched her friend and neighbor for several minutes. She noticed that Moria seemed happy. Her smile was genuine, not forced as it used to be. She had a glow about her that showed Nancy that she was very healthy and happy.

"Children," she shouted over her shoulder, "Ronan's here to play!"

Immediately Moria could hear a cheer from a few of the kids as they came from the other room. Moria slowly lowered Ronan to the floor and watched as the children played gently with Ronan.

"Nancy," Moria began. "I don't know if you heard the news, but the king has left on a journey. We have no idea how long he is going to be gone."

Nancy looked surprised. "What happened to the young lady everyone thought he was going to marry?"

Moria smiled. "Well, that's the reason he's gone. He went back to his father to prepare a place for her. When he returns, there will be a great marriage celebration."

"You mean the king has left us entirely? That's bad news Moria."

"No, Nancy, listen. He is coming back to marry Sine once everything is ready. I think that's great news."

Nancy's expression still did not change. "Moria, that means that he will marry Sine and leave us."

Suddenly Moria realized what Nancy was saying. That's why Marcus was so excited that he was asked to oversee the daily goings on of the kingdom.

"Oh, I had not thought of that," Moria said almost too quietly to be heard.

Suddenly she did not like the idea of change. *I don't know if I can make the castle my home, how would I raise a young child with all that commotion?* Moria tried not to think about that right now.

Pushing the thought out of her head she said, "Nancy, the reason I came to tell you that, was because, with the king gone, he has asked Marcus to move to the castle. It is only temporary to tend to the needs of the people. I have packed up the items in my house that I thought I would need, but I wanted to offer you the fruits of my garden."

"Thank you, Moria," Nancy said, "Those vegetables will not be wasted. I greatly appreciate your generosity. I will keep my eye on the house also for when or if you return."

"What do you mean 'If'?" Moria pressed Nancy with the question.

"Moria, have you thought about the fact that Cullen may make Marcus the leader of Dia Richoet? You may move to the castle permanently."

Moria looked at the children playing in the other room. "Yes, I have thought about that. I am not going to allow myself to get upset by that thought, yet. Perhaps that won't happen, or perhaps I will like living in the castle. I'll let you know as time goes by." Moria smiled at her friend. "Nancy, I will visit you often."

Moria noticed the expression on Nancy's face. Her eyes sparkled like she knew a secret and Moria just wasn't telling. "What are you looking at me like that for?" Moria asked.

Nancy chuckled. "Moria, are your hiding something from me?"

Again, Moria noticed how her eyes danced. "Okay, I am but how did you know?"

Nancy's chuckled, "That is something I just know. I can tell."

Moria was surprised. "But I haven't even told you my surprise, yet. How could you possibly know what it is?"

Nancy 's expression was thoughtful. "You are with child, aren't you?"

Moria could hardly believe her ears. Moria had known for several weeks now, but she had not told anyone not even Marcus. Moria still did not respond to Nancy's question she just stared at her in disbelief.

"Dear girl," Nancy started, "I have helped so many women with childbirth, not to mention I have five children of my own, I notice the little subtle signs like your headaches, aching back and fatigue. You came to me last week to ask if I had any White Willow Bark. You have mentioned how potent the flowers smell, yet, I can barely smell them. Not to mention that twinkle in your eye." Nancy picked Ronan up from the floor and looked Moria in the eyes. "Let me just say I am glad you look much healthier and stronger than you did when you had Ronan."

"Please don't tell anyone, yet, Nancy," Moria said. "I haven't even told Marcus."

Ronan began squirming in Nancy's arms when he saw one of Nancy's children. Nancy placed Ronan on the floor to play with her daughter.

"He was so worried when Ronan was born. I am not sure how he will take the news."

"You act like you are feeling better with this pregnancy, am I right?"

"Yes, I am not weak or even very sick. I mostly have the headaches and the sore back. Sometimes I am sick in the morning, but nothing severe. I'm having a hard time trying to figure out how to talk to Marcus about it. I want him happy, not concerned."

"I wouldn't tell. It is not my place, but I am happy for the two of you."

After a few hours of talking, and dreaming about the new baby on the way, and life in a castle Moria picked up the now very tired Ronan and said her goodbyes.

"Don't forget to harvest those vegetables, Nancy," Moria said as she was heading out the door.

"I won't," Nancy replied, "Thanks again for the food. Don't forget to visit often. I'll miss seeing you. You can't leave me a lonely old woman now." She said with a smile.

Moria laughed, "Nancy, I can't imagine you lonely or old. You have such a loving family you will never be alone, and you have a long way to go before you're old."

Training

Ever since the day that Marcus reminded Sine she could still communicate with Cullen, she made it a habit of talking with him each day before she got out of bed. *Good morning Cullen.*

Good morning. How are you doing? Now that Sine had learned to listen, Cullen's voice was clear and loud, as if he was standing in the same room.

I am okay, she thought, *but I really miss seeing you. When are you coming back?* Sine sat in silence for a few minutes.

Sine, you know I don't know the time that I am returning. I have told you that many times. I need to wait for my father to send me.

Sine felt embarrassed for asking her question. *I know,* she thought, *I'm just getting tired of not seeing you. Cullen, I love you very much. Thank you for getting me free from King Dorcha and bringing me here to safety. I have never imagined such love.*

Again, there was silence. This time the period of silence was a little lengthier than usual.

Sine. Sine could sense the frustration in Cullen's voice. *Sine, you tell me every day that you love me. Are you sure those words are true?*

Sine felt as if she was punched in the stomach. *Cullen, of course, I love you! I thank you each morning for saving me, and I tell you every day that I love you!*

Sine, have you done what I asked? Cullen's voice was gentle as he continued. *Sine, I have asked you to do two critical things. First, I asked you to befriend the villagers and tell them about me. Secondly, I have asked you to train for battle. In our conversations, you talk to me all about how much you miss me. You have never mentioned that you are training, and you have never told me about your new friends in the village. If you truly loved me, show it by doing what I have asked you to do.*

Sine squeezed her eyes shut to stop the tears that were threatening to fall. *I am so sorry Cullen,* she thought, *you are right; I haven't been doing either of those things. I am just too scared.*

Sine, your love for me should help you overcome your fears.

Very well, she said, *I will start today.*

As Sine ate her breakfast a sense of foreboding hung in the air around her. *How am I going to do this? Why am I so scared? Marcus is a friend, I will ask to begin my training. Later I will go to the village.*

Marcus stood in the grand hall looking over all the people who had gathered. The number was too vast they could not all fit in the room. The crowd of people overflowed into the courtyard.

"Good people of Dia Richoet, I have requested all who are loyal to the king meet me here in the Great Room. It is good to see so many people love King Cullen."

"Long live King Cullen!" The shout went out from the people in one voice like a deafening roar.

"The king requested that in his absence I train you all how to bear arms." The murmurings began within the crowd. "Good people of Dia Richoet!" Marcus now needed to shout to be heard. "There is no need to fear; he just wants us to be prepared and aware of our enemy, King Dorcha. Please give your names to my men, and I will visit each house separately. Then I can answer any questions you may have."

Marcus watched as his soldiers talked with the people. He thought, *Cullen, I wonder if you knew what a job you're asking me to do.* Marcus went to find his wife; he wanted her company. Something about being around her made him feel refreshed. Talking to the villagers was draining him emotionally. Yes, many had feared, but many were staying loyal to the king. As Marcus was walking down the long corridors of the castle, he heard someone calling his name.

"Marcus?"

He turned to see Sine walking toward him holding Ronan. Once Sine got closer to Marcus she noticed the tense expression on his face. His skin was pale, and his eyes were slightly sunken and darker as if he had not slept in days.

"Marcus, you don't look too good, are you doing okay?"

Irritated that he was being interrupted, he gruffly said, "I'll be fine." The truth was he was not mad at all, just tired of trying to explain to the villagers why they should not be afraid and training them was proving to be an enormous task.

"Cullen told me that he asked you to teach me archery. I promise I will do my best and try my hardest," Sine said.

Marcus smiled a weak smile. "Thanks, Sine, I have a lot of people to teach. It will be refreshing to work with someone who is trying their best to do what the king requested."

"Just tell me when my training will begin," Sine said.

Marcus let out a deep sigh. "I'll start training you next week. Get plenty of rest; you will need it."

Marcus walked into the room he now called home. As much as he loved living in the castle, sometimes he missed the simplicity of his cottage in the country. Closing the door behind him, he called "Moria?"

"Yes, sweetheart," her voice rang out from the room adjacent to where he was standing.

"You sound very cheerful."

Moria came around the corner with a smile on her face. "Oh, Marcus, you look exhausted. Did things not go well with the villagers?"

Marcus slowly sank into the closest chair. "Well, they didn't go that badly, but this is going to be a lot of work. Many people are worried but are going to try their hardest. Even Sine is willing to be trained. I am only one man, how am I going to train them all?" He looked up at Moria and remembered her cheerful mood when he first walked in. "Never mind all that, it's not your concern. Tell me about your day. You sure were cheerful when I first walked in. Don't let my troubles change your mood."

Moria smiled "Well, I am concerned about you and your day."

"I know you are, but please tell me about your day."

Again, Moria smiled, "Well, I packed up the things in the house I figured I would need while we stayed at the castle. Then I visited with Nancy. I told her to harvest my vegetable garden while I was away." Moria could feel the heat rising in her face. Marcus noticed the rosy complexion on her face.

"What is it? Moria you look embarrassed."

Moria chuckled, "Oh, I'm not embarrassed ..." she said, her eyes dancing with excitement. "I'm with child!"

Marcus couldn't believe what he was hearing. "What! We are going to have another child?! Moria are you sure?" Moria just nodded her head excitedly. Marcus' mind was racing. Things were so difficult for her with Ronan. Was this a good thing? "Moria, I'm happy for us, but I'm scared too. I almost lost you when you had Ronan." Moria understood what he was trying to say.

"Marcus, I am much stronger and healthier now. This pregnancy doesn't feel anything like how I felt with Ronan. I'm sure it will be okay."

Marcus held her in a strong embrace. "I sure hope your right. A baby is such a joyous treasure, but I couldn't stand losing you."

No matter how hard she tried, Sine just could not imagine holding or using a weapon. *I hate fighting,* she thought to herself. *Why can't people just get along?* Sine stared out the window to the village in the distance. *Will we even need to fight?* She wasn't sure why she felt so sad at the thought of fighting. *Chances are, we would never go to war with*

anyone, right? Everyone she met was very peaceful and happy. *I'll do my best as I promised,* she thought, *Cullen was just over concerned.*

A week had passed since Sine spoke with Marcus. Today marked the beginning of her training. As she ate breakfast, Marcus approached her.

"Meet me in the garden in an hour," he said, then turned abruptly and left the room.

He's been acting so strange lately. I hope he is alright. Sine thought to herself as she watched him leave the room.

As Sine walked into the garden, she saw that Marcus was already waiting there for her. "Sorry if I am late," she said.

"No, you're not late. I was early." He abruptly turned and handed her a bow. "Here's your bow. I want you to carry it everywhere with you. It is not a heavy weapon, and you can easily slide it over your shoulder, so your hands are free. I don't ever want to see you without this bow. Understand?"

Sine thought, *He sure is tough. I don't think this will be friendly training.* "Yes, I understand, but why the urgency?"

Marcus looked at Sine. "Sine, I'm sorry if I am coming across as harsh. There is no urgency right now. I just want you protected at all times. The faster you learn to shoot, the quicker I will relax."

Sine felt herself relax when she heard his words. "Marcus, you're a great warrior. I am sure I will learn quickly from your teaching."

Marcus' expression told her that he was not so sure. "Good, then let's begin," he said with a slight smile.

"Okay, let's see what you can do. Lift your bow, taking the arrow, place this end against the string and pull back as far as you can. Let the shaft of the arrow just rest against the bow."

Sine tried her best to pull hard on the string and do all that Marcus was instructing her to, but she knew he wanted her to pull back on the line harder.

"Ok, good. Now focus on the target. When you think your arrow is lined up, release it."

Sine did as she was told. As she released her hold on the string, she felt a stinging, burning sensation as the shaft slid against her hand. Sine was disappointed that the arrow did not make it very far and definitely did not reach the target.

"Well," Marcus began, "You have a lot of potential. I have trained soldiers who cannot shoot that far on the first try."

Sine could barely believe what Marcus was saying. "You mean I did better than you thought? I didn't even make it to the target?"

Marcus chuckled. "You mean you expected to get a perfect shot the first time you ever held a bow?"

Sine felt embarrassed. "Well, yeah! I told you I would try my best."

"With that determination. I know you will."

They continued to work for the next three hours. Sine's arm was sore; the muscles were burning in her upper arm. The arrow that would scrape across the top of her hand left her hand red and bleeding

Marcus was impressed by her sheer determination to learn. *Cullen, I wish you could see Sine now, you would be very proud of her,* he thought to himself. Marcus noticed her hands were getting raw. Several times he offered to let her stop the lesson early, each time she refused.

"I told you I would try my best, quitting now wouldn't be my best, now would it?" Sine said with determination.

"Tomorrow, I want you to go to the royal stables and help clean them. Lifting and shoveling will strengthen your arms. I know you will be sore in the morning, but if you press through the pain, it will get better."

Several days had passed, and now it was another day of training for Sine. The sores on her hands were not healed, and her arms felt as if there was no strength left in them. *How am I going to do another lesson today?* She thought. As she made her way to the garden to meet Marcus, she hoped she would be able to hold the bow tight enough to be able to pull the string back.

"Well, I wasn't sure if you would come," Marcus said when he saw her enter the garden.

"Why?"

"Many people want to quit. They are all complaining that this training is too much work. They think it's a job for the soldiers only."

Sine looked at the blisters and sores on her hands. "Well, they definitely hurt, but I'm here."

Marcus approached with a small leather piece in his hands. "Good. Otherwise, the leather smith would have wasted his time making this. Hold out your right hand."

Sine winced as he carefully slid the leather over her hand. It fit like a tight glove.

"Now, this will prevent the arrow from cutting your skin. Let's see how it works."

Gingerly, Sine took an arrow from the quiver and mounted it tightly against the string. As Sine pulled back on the bow, her arm quivered. She focused on the target and released the arrow. Once again it fell short of the mark.

"How did that feel?" Marcus asked, "Did that prevent the arrow from cutting into your hand?"

"Yes," she said quietly. Sine could tell that she sounded discouraged. "I'm sorry I feel so weak."

Marcus looked frustrated. "Sine, stop that. You're going to be tired after everything you did. Don't be so hard on yourself. We won't work for three hours today. We will keep it short."

Again, Sine drew an arrow from the quiver and placed it in the bow. Marcus stood by Sine's right side. "You need to keep your elbow in, close to your side."

Sine tucked her elbow close to her body.

"Yes, that's right. Now you will have more control. Now pull back."

Sine could feel her arm quivering. Marcus noticed it too, but he chose not to say anything. He would take it easy on her today. The next training session he would show her how to hold the sword. That would use different muscles in her arm and give her upper arm a rest.

That night as Sine laid in bed, she allowed the tears to come. *Oh, Cullen* she groaned, *I'm sorry, I don't think I can do this.* The more Sine thought of her failure, the harder the tears fell. Amid her tears, she heard Cullen's voice.

I know this is difficult for you, but more importantly, I know you can do it.

Sine's heart beat faster in her chest just to hear his voice again. *Cullen, you don't understand! I am trying as hard as I can! I honestly didn't think it would be this difficult. I can barely move, and when I think I am doing better, my arrow hardly makes it halfway to the target!*

Cullen's voice rang out as clear as if he was standing next to her. *Sine, I would never ask you to do something that you cannot do. Don't worry, you will become a great warrior. I know it.*

Sine just could not get her mind to agree with the words Cullen was telling her. Feeling utterly defeated, Sine cried until the tears would no longer come. Soon she fell into a deep sleep from exhaustion.

The Villagers

Good morning, Cullen! She waited a moment to hear Cullen's reply.

Good morning.

Cullen, she thought, *I am sorry I can't shoot the arrow. Why did you ever think I could?*

Don't get tired of trying. I know you will get it soon. Perhaps you should give yourself a break from the arrow and go visit the village.

At first, Sine felt very uncomfortable with the idea. But the more she thought about it, the more excited she became.

After breakfast, Sine Headed down the path to the nearest village. Sine paid attention to the beauty that surrounded her. It was a beautiful sunny Summer morning the air temperature was perfect for walking. Sine took a deep breath of fresh morning air. Today she had determined that she was going to make the best of it and go to the village to meet some of the villagers. As soon as she walked into the marketplace, she took a step back just to watch and observe the people.

She noticed an old woman in the marketplace whose hands were crippled from years of weaving baskets the wrinkles on her face show that she spent many years in the sun. Sine thought, *now that is a woman I would like to meet.* With a boldness that she didn't even know she had she said,

"Hello my name is Sine. What is your name?"

The woman looked up with old gray eyes her hair was white and wispy and unruly even though it was pulled back into a bun.

"Why should you care about who I am?" The old woman said with anger in her voice. "I know you; you're from the castle. You think you're somebody special just because the king loves you. Well, let me tell you, you're nobody special at all. Just a pretty face."

Sine was shocked at the answer. At first, she wanted to defend herself and tell this old woman she had no business talking to her like that, but then she remembered her past. She remembered how she used to believe that lie.

"I am sorry that you feel that way," Sine said, "Truth is you don't know me very well, and you definitely don't know the king at all."

The old woman looked at her with criticizing eyes. "Who are you to tell me that I don't know the king? I have lived in this village my whole life I think by now I know the king."

Sine thought for a moment. "The king is gracious; he is kind and very loving. The love he has for all of his people is greater and deeper than I can comprehend."

The old woman sneered, "If his love is so good, why do I have these troubles in my life? Why did my husband die when he was young? Why did both of my children die? Now I live, barely making it by weaving baskets; soon my old hands won't be able to weave another basket. What am I to do then? The king loves me, huh? What kind of love is that?"

Sine was taken off guard by what the woman had said. "I am sorry, my lady; it sounds like you had a tough life. However, the king is not responsible for all those things. Is he even aware that you are struggling to make it just by weaving baskets? Does he know you? I can see that years of basket weaving has crippled your hands. It must be challenging for you to weave baskets. Have you ever told the king that you cannot continue to weave baskets to make a living? Does he know you have no family to help you?"

Now the old woman seemed a little embarrassed. "No! Why would I bother the king with my problems and he wouldn't care, anyhow?"

"Oh. but that is where you are wrong!" Sine went on to tell her that King Cullen really wants all the villagers to come to him with their needs and their problems. "He really wants to help. Please, tell him who you are and what your needs are."

The old woman seemed a little reluctant to agree, but she finally nodded her head and said, "you are one persistent woman."

"Oh, I am sorry," Sine said, "I just remembered King Cullen is on a journey. I do not know when he will return, but you can still go the castle and ask to see Marcus. He has been instructed to take care of the king's business until King Cullen returns."

"I will try I will visit the castle and make my requests known, I still have a hard time believing anyone would care about an old woman and her problems."

Sine smiled, "you will not be disappointed. The king is a very generous and kind man."

Preparing for War

Marcus could tell that Sine needed a small break from the archery lessons. He decided to give her a few days rest and focus his training with some of the other villagers who were remaining loyal to King Cullen. Today he was going to work with Patrick. Patrick had an advantage that many of the villagers did not have. Since his work as a stone cutter, required great strength Patrick was already very fit and ready to become a skilled warrior. Marcus knew if he made him skillful with the sword, he would fight well. He was indeed a warrior in Marcus's eyes.

Patrick was already waiting for Marcus in the courtyard when he arrived.

"Well, someone looks eager this morning," Marcus said enthusiastically, as he came toward Patrick.

"Yes, my lord, I am ready for my lesson," he said as he turned to face Marcus.

Marcus noticed the angle of the sun's rays as the sun crested the hill displaying a beautiful sunrise.

"Well, then let's get ready for a good friendly dual," Marcus said as he unsheathed his sword.

Patrick's expression told Marcus that he was not expecting to duel his teacher on his first lesson, but he drew his sword anyway. Marcus smiled to remind his new friend that this was just a friendly dual. As he flashed his sword at just the right angle, he caught the morning's sunlight shining directly into Patrick's eyes, making it impossible for Patrick to see clearly. In a panic, Patrick started to swing his sword as if he could see his opposition.

"Come on, Patrick," Marcus said with a chuckle, "What are you trying to do with that sword of yours? I know you can't see me, I could have easily killed you a few times over by now."

Patrick was still blindly swinging his sword as if he was fighting an imaginary opponent.

"Patrick, use your head," Marcus said calmly, "If I am blinding you with the sunlight, what do you need to do to change the direction I am standing in? Change my position, the blinding light will stop, and you may be able to use the sun to your advantage."

Patrick stopped swinging his sword in the air. "I don't know," he said meekly.

"Patrick, I know you're smarter than that. Think! Think as if your life depends on it. Someday it might."

Patrick lifted his sword and began swinging in the direction the light was coming from. This time, however, he walked toward the right. Soon, he had turned Marcus's direction enough that the sun was no longer able to be reflected on Marcus' blade.

"Very good," Marcus said, "but you would have died a long time ago. You need to make sure that you are never distracted by the enemy. Always look for the upper hand or the advantage. When I first walked into this courtyard to fight with you, I had already judged where I should stand to take advantage of the sunrise. I will teach you to look for the upper hand every time you are forced to fight."

Marcus decided to challenge Patrick with the strength of his arm and sword fighting skills. As they began to duel, Marcus was impressed by Patrick's power, but he was very sloppy with the sword.

"Patrick, you seem to be trying too hard. Relax. You will be at a great disadvantage if you begin to panic." Marcus continued, "Look, your swings are too wide. When you over swing like that, you leave yourself wide open for a direct hit. Keep your sword closer to your body that will prevent any opening for the enemy to stab at you."

They continued to duel together for a while. Slowly, Patrick's strength began to fail. Marcus was surprised as he watched Patrick. He was wheezing and gasping. Marcus stopped the training and watched Patrick as he tried his best to catch his breath.

"Well, it looks like the first measure of business we have, is to get you into shape. You are very strong, but your endurance is lacking," Marcus chuckled, "Let's start with a run first thing in the morning. We will meet here in the courtyard, you can join several others who need to build their strength. We all begin running at sunrise each day. Then, after our run, we will challenge each other with different activities to strengthen our bodies more than just running. I will recommend that you train with the sword for several hours each day."

Patrick was looking very tired. His face was red; his hair was wet with perspiration. The perspiration that had been beading up on his forehead was now running down the sides of his face. "Yes, I guess I need to get into shape fast," He gasped, "I had no idea I couldn't keep up with you. I thought I would be pretty good at this." He gave Marcus a crooked smile. "Please stop today's training while I still have a tiny bit of dignity left."

"That's what I like about you, Patrick." Marcus smiled. "You can carry a good sense of humor even when you have been soundly defeated. So, I will see you at first light, tomorrow right?"

"Yes, sir," Patrick groaned, "First light. If I can get my sore body out of bed that is."

"Oh, you will, or I will personally come get your sore body out of bed and believe me, you will be much more aware of your aches and pains if I have to come and get you." Marcus enjoyed teasing his friend. He would never be that hard on Patrick, but Patrick didn't know Marcus well enough yet to be aware that he was only teasing. "In the meantime, go home, put some Ice on those sore muscles of yours. Later, apply some comforting heat. Don't forget to eat some red meat. That will help your muscles recover faster." He turned to face Patrick, and with a smile, he said, "It's not like I want to see you in pain, I just want to see you stronger, so you don't get hurt if you're ever in battle my friend."

A Sword for Sine

It was early morning several minutes before sunrise. Sine lay in bed wishing morning would not come. Her body was sore from all the training; she had barely slept that entire night. Sine decided to turn her thoughts toward Cullen. *Cullen, how I wish you were here. I have tried my best to learn how to shoot the arrow well. I really want to do better, but I feel like such a failure.* Sine stopped to listen, but silence was all she heard.

Now the sun was rising enough that the early morning light was beginning to fill her room. There was a knock on her door.

"Yes," Sine called, "Come in."

Sine was surprised that anyone would disturb her at this hour in the morning. Slowly the door opened, and a very timid maid peered her head into the room.

"I am sorry to bother you, my lady, but Marcus asked for your presence in the courtyard."

"At this hour? Doesn't he believe in a little rest?"

Sine watched the young girl; it was apparent that she was uncomfortable with the whole idea of waking Sine up to deliver her message.

"I am sorry, my lady; I am only following orders," she said quietly.

Not wanting the girl to feel any more uncomfortable than she already was Sine sat up in bed as she said. "Fine, please tell Marcus I will be there shortly."

The young girl silently closed the door as she said, "Yes ma'am."

Sine was met with the brilliant sunlight as she walked into the courtyard. Marcus noticed her coming toward him and turned to meet her.

"Good morning, sleepy head," Marcus said in a teasing tone. "We missed you for our morning run."

Sine involuntarily groaned. "I am sorry, I completely forgot you had asked me to arrive before sunlight. Honestly, I just wanted to keep sleeping. How long can I keep going like this? I am exhausted!" She said as he began rubbing her sore arms.

"Sine, I have different plans for you today. I know are getting tired and sore from shooting the bow, so I figured I would teach you about how to fight with a sword, instead."

Marcus studied her expression as he spoke. He watched as her expression slowly turned from relief to concern and even shock. Sine still had not said a word; she was having a difficult time believing what she had just heard Marcus say.

"Sine?"

It was as if his voice woke her up. The look of disbelief was clearly marked on her face.

"You mean to tell me that you plan on teaching me to sword fight?!" Her voice sounded high and squeaky as if she had run out of air while she was talking.

Marcus knew he needed to quickly reassure her before fear took the place of her disbelief. "Sine, you don't know what your strengths are, yet. You may enjoy sword fighting better than the bow."

"You say that, but I think you're wrong. I probably won't even be able to hold a sword never mind swing one!" Sine could hear her voice getting louder. Frustrated she shouted, "Marcus, I am simply not that strong! Don't you understand?"

Sine was surprised at Marcus' response. He merely smiled as he showed her the sword and sheath he had been holding behind his back. Sine noticed that the sword was much thinner than his sword and it was longer and looked like it might be something she could learn to handle.

"That is why I had this sword especially crafted for you. It is lightweight but extremely sharp. Learn how to handle this, and you will be more than able to protect yourself. Come on, your lessons begin now."

Sine willed her fear to subside as she cautiously took the sword from Marcus' hands. Immediately the weight of the sword surprised her. Just as Marcus said, it was very light. As she sliced through the air at an imaginary foe, it felt as if the sword had a mind of its own.

"Well, what do you think?" Marcus' question surprised Sine. "Is it too heavy? Or is it something you're willing to try?"

Sine looked at Marcus. He was not mocking her as she thought he would. After a moment she humbly said, "I will try it." The idea of fighting with a sword seemed to be more appealing than the bow. Suddenly the thought of fighting someone like Philip entered her mind.

"Although," she hesitated. "I don't want to fight anyone close up. What if I have to fight someone who is very strong and a skilled swordsman."

"Sine, you can't worry about those types of things. You need to be prepared in case you should need to fight. That's all you should be thinking about right now," Marcus replied as he encouragingly placed his hand on her shoulder "Sine, you are a powerful, wise, beloved bride. No matter how difficult challenges become you must attack them with boldness and confidence." Silently he turned and began walking toward a bench that was located near the castle wall. "Come and sit while I explain things to you. Today I won't work you too hard; there is a lot I want to teach you before you ever swing that sword."

Sine sat on the bench as Marcus requested and leaned her back against the castle wall. The idea of not working extremely hard today sounded great to her, she was determined to listen carefully, or Marcus may change his mind and teach her by working with her. Marcus stood facing her his sword still in his sheaf as he began speaking.

"The most important thing you need to learn about sword fighting is really true for any type of fighting." With a sweeping motion, Marcus gestured with his hand in the direction of the courtyard. "Be very aware of your surroundings you will need to learn how to take in your environment and know how to use them to your advantage. If you ever have the feeling that something is wrong, trust your instinct. When I was training Patrick the other day, I explained to him how he can use things like the sunlight to blind his opponent or if not careful; your opponent can blind you. Pay attention to barriers like walls and cliffs. You can use them to help you or your opponent may try to use them to surprise attack you. If you ever fight a soldier who is wearing heavy armor, you may be able to trap him if you can lure him into the mud."

Marcus spoke for several hours. During that time, he showed Sine how to stand to keep balanced and the best way to position her arms. Marcus was true to his word, he had not worked Sine too hard, and she appreciated the break.

"Tomorrow, I will give you a small lesson in the correct way to engage with your opponent. But mostly I will challenge you with your environment. I hope you were paying attention." He smiled. "Now, I'll let you take the remainder of the day off."

Family

Marcus turned his horse toward the castle. He was tired and had worked up a good appetite. *Nothing that a good meal and a little rest could not help.* He thought. Marcus had not spent much time with Moria or Ronan these last few weeks and was looking forward to seeing them tonight. Tomorrow early in the morning, he would be training again, but he was not planning to be away the entire day. He needed to stay in the Throne Room and take care of some of the problems that had come to his attention.

After dinner, Marcus sat and watched Ronan as he played on the floor. Just recently, Ronan had pulled himself up to a standing position. Marcus was very disappointed that he had missed seeing Ronan's accomplishment. As Marcus sat watching his son, Ronan used his round fingers to grasp the table that was in the middle of the room. With a struggle, he began to pull himself to stand. Marcus watched as he gave up and sat back down on the floor.

"You can do it," Marcus coached, "it's Okay. Come on, try again."

Ronan grasped the table again and slowly pulled to try to stand. Still, his chubby legs wouldn't support him, and he felt back to the floor, this time tipping over and lightly bumping his head on the wooden floor. Ronan sat on the floor, his face wrinkled up into a mournful cry.

"It's okay," Marcus said, silently willing Ronan not to cry. "You can do it."

Ronan looked at Marcus as if he understood what Marcus had said, slowly the tension in his face that showed he was about to cry relaxed. Once again, Marcus watched as Ronan tried to stand for the third time.

"I think he gets that determination from you. You never give up on a situation no matter how hopeless it seems."

Moria's voice startled Marcus. Not wanting to take his eyes off his son, he glanced over his shoulder. Moria was standing in the doorway behind him, and her eyes were full of love.

"I mean, look at us, I was ready to give up, but you had such a determination to save our relationship ..." Moria's words stopped short as her eyes were fastened on Ronan.

Marcus turned to see what Moria had been looking at when she stopped so abruptly. Just then Ronan pulled himself to a stand holding onto the table.

"Yeah, Ronan!" Marcus cheered. "I knew you could do it!"

Ronan's smile spread across his chubby face as he turned to look at his father. He took a wobbly step toward Marcus, but he still hung on to the table with both hands. He was only a short distance from Marcus but would need to release his grasp on the table to reach his father.

"Well, this is as far as he has gone," Moria said, "He refuses to let go of that table."

"Good boy!" Marcus encouraged him. "You can do it! Walk to your father."

Ronan's smile left his face as he looked at the floor. The distance between him and his father must have seemed very far. Ronan looked back up at Marcus. His expression showed that he was scared.

Marcus leaned forward in his chair and reached forward with both arms outstretched toward Ronan to shorten the distance between Ronan and himself.

"Come on buddy; I know you can do it."

Slowly, as if someone were prying his fingers off the table, Ronan let go of the table and took a step toward Marcus. His first step was deliberate, but the two steps that followed looked more like he had tripped and was trying not to fall. Immediately Marcus scooped him up into his arms and let out a shout.

"Moria! Did you see that! He walked to me!"

Marcus was overjoyed because he was able to not only see his son's first steps, but Ronan walked to him. Ronan was laughing in his arms, and Moria was joining in with the celebration. Remembering what Moria had just said about not giving up, he got a little more serious as he looked at Moria.

"Moria, I would never give this up. Not you or Ronan. I love you both so much; you're my life. I can't imagine ever being without either of you." Marcus turned and kissed Moria. "Don't ever think anything else. As far as that determination you were talking about." Marcus kissed her again and looked deep into her eyes. "I would give everything I have to keep you and Ronan. I will never leave you or Ronan. Not now, not ever."

A short time later, Moria put Ronan to bed. It had been a tiring day for the child, and he was asleep almost immediately. Moria came into the living room and sat next to Marcus.

"So, tell me, how are things going with the training? I feel like I haven't seen you for days!"

Marcus turned to look at his beloved Moria. Things sure had changed this last year. It seemed like just the other day she was telling him to leave. Her heart was so bitter and angry after she had given birth to Ronan that Marcus thought the Moria he loved was gone for good. A smile spread across his lips as he took in her beauty. The light of the fire was gently dancing across her face. Her eyes were peaceful, and her expression was happy again.

"Training is going well." Marcus thought back to his day with Patrick. "Many of the men need to work extra hard to be ready to fight, but the spirits are good. Everyone is willing to try their best, which surprises me. Remember when I first talked to the men about training? Almost all of them complained. It is good to see the attitudes are changing."

"I wonder what changed their minds?" Moria was staring into the fireplace. She looked deep in thought. "Did you talk with them more?"

"Remember, I met with each one separately. I tried my best to encourage each able villager. I showed them their strengths, not their weaknesses. Perhaps that's what did it. I don't know." Marcus' expression became serious. "We still have a long way to go. I hope we will be ready. Many men have lost their loyalty to King Cullen. They refuse to prepare for war."

"Don't talk like that!" Moria seemed surprised by Marcus' downcast attitude. "Marcus, I know you're doing your best. You're the best commander anywhere. That's why Cullen trusts you to do this task!"

"What if Cullen was wrong," Marcus was staring at the floor he had not been able to share his true feelings with anyone, and now that he was voicing them he felt even more defeated. He turned and looked at Moria; his eyes were raw with emotion. Immediately he turned and looked at the floor again. "I don't want to fail the king, Moria. What if I can't do what he's asking?"

Moria felt frustrated she wasn't sure how she could encourage Marcus. She had never seen him so discouraged.

Marcus looked at Moria. "Moria, I know you are good at archery, but I want you to practice more. Perhaps you can practice with Sine."

"Do you think there is a danger?" Moria was trying her best not to show the alarm that was attempting to put fear in her spirit.

"There won't be any danger if we are prepared. It's just that if a war begins, I won't be able to stay with you and Ronan. I want you to be protected."

Moria was trying desperately to control her racing mind. *"Don't panic, don't panic. It will be okay,"* she told herself, *"Marcus won't leave me if a battle starts, will he?"*

Marcus could tell by the look in Moria's eyes that she was fearful. "Moria, I didn't mean to scare you. Chances are you will not ever see fighting or be involved in any fight. I just want you to remember how to fight in case you should need to. Besides, it will encourage Sine if she has someone to train with that is a woman. She is comparing herself to me, and that is not right. Sine gets discouraged easily when she cannot shoot as far as I can. Please, just practice with her."

Moria silently nodded in agreement. She felt the weight of what Marcus was telling her. He would have to leave her to go to war if a battle started. "Marcus, I can't stand the thought of war. I will train as you requested, but please, tell me that this battle is not going to happen. I can't stand the thought of losing you in a fight." She felt the tears burning her eyes, but she refused to let them come. The fear quickly turned to anger. "Besides!" She jumped to her feet. "You just promised me that you would never leave me!"

Marcus stood and leveled Moria's gaze. His eyes were not angry, but she knew he was not going to allow her to argue with him. "Yes, I did just say that. I don't plan on leaving you." Marcus said with his expression unwavering. "But I also said I would give everything I had for you. If I were to die in battle, it would be to protect you and Ronan."

Moria could not hold back the tears any longer. As they spilled silently down her face, she begged, "Marcus, please don't talk like that."

Marcus pulled her into an embrace and held her until her tears stopped. "Moria, don't get upset now. We are not at war and Cullen will be returning soon. He told me when he returns he will bring King Domnall's army. We will be undefeatable then. I will fight alongside Cullen, but you are not to fear. I have fought with him in many battles, and you were never this scared before. Be at peace, my dear."

Moria and Sine had spent many weeks together in the garden as Moria practiced her archery giving Sine instructions and encouragement. No matter how much support Moria gave, Sine just felt like a failure. Today, Marcus was going to train her.

"Marcus," Sine began. "I have been trying to learn from Moria, but I just can't seem to shoot. My arm isn't strong enough. I still can't even reach the target. I don't think I will ever be able to do this." Sine sounded defeated. She looked at the ground as she spoke, nervously kicking pebbles that were laying on the ground.

"Sine, when you discredit yourself by not believing you're going to become a great warrior, you are also dishonoring Cullen. The king knows you are more than a conqueror."

Sine thought about those words for a moment. "I never thought about it like that," she said quietly, "I don't want to dishonor Cullen, but I don't care about discrediting myself. I know I am nothing special."

Marcus looked at Sine and noticed how she even looked defeated. "Sine, I think that is something you should talk with Cullen about. I know he would disagree with you. I know this has been hard, but you have been doing well."

Sine shook her head in agreement. "Okay, I will talk with Cullen later," she said fully knowing Marcus was right. Cullen would definitely tell her how much he valued her. As much as she knew that was how Cullen felt, she had such a difficult time believing it.

"Excellent!" Marcus said with a smile, "Now focus on the target and release."

Sine let the arrow fly.

"Yeah!" Marcus shouted so loud it startled Sine.

She looked and saw that her arrow reached the target! She was nowhere near reaching the middle of the goal, but at least it went far enough.

"Sine you did it!"

"I can't believe it," she whispered, "I actually hit the target?"

Marcus' eyes were dancing. "Even though your arms are tired, you were able to reach the target! That's great!"

Marcus' excitement made Sine smile, he really did want to see her become an excellent marksman.

Hannah

Moria was amazed by the difference in this pregnancy compared to when she was pregnant with Ronan. With Ronan, she was always tired and had excruciating pain in her abdomen. For months before Ronan was born Moria was afraid to do the simplest tasks. Getting out of bed was a challenge in itself.

This pregnancy was completely different. From the very first month when Moria knew she was with child, she knew this child would be different. Throughout the first couple months, Moria did not experience sickness very much in the morning. And her strength did not fade as the day progresses. Moria had even been able to practice her archery skills and teach Sine as Marcus had asked her to. That may have only been for a few weeks, but Moria knew she never would have been able to do that when she was pregnant with Ronan. As she got closer to delivering the baby, Moria could tell she was getting stronger.

This winter had been a mild one. Moria was able to go for walks on a daily basis. She bundled Ronan up in a warm cloak. "Come on buddy," Moria said as Ronan let out a happy cry. "My hips seem to have disappeared" she chuckled to herself. "It's harder to carry you, my little buddy. Let's see if Sine would like to come for a walk with us." Ronan let out another happy squeal. Quickly Moria left her quarters with Ronan and set out to find Sine.

Sine had practiced early that morning with Patrick. Although she liked fighting with the sword much better than the arrow, she didn't like the idea of one on one combat. As she came into the courtyard, she saw Moria heading her way.

"Sine!" Moria shouted.

Sine put her sword back in its sheaf and began walking toward Moria. "Hello Moria, you look cheerful today, are you and Ronan going somewhere?"

"Honestly, that depends on you. I was going to ask if you would please come with Ronan and I as we go for our daily walk. I can not carry Ronan very much anymore. The baby makes it difficult to put Ronan on my hip."

Sine was cautious. "Isn't the baby due to come very soon?"

"Sine, I am fine. Never felt better. I don't think the baby is coming today. Please, I really want to get some fresh air, and I know Marcus would not want me to go off on my own."

"I would be happy to accompany you and Ronan," Sine said with a smile, "I love being with Ronan he's such a happy boy. Here, let me take him from you," she said as she reached her hands toward the boy. Ronan immediately reached his chubby hands and leaned his whole weight towards Sine forcing Moria to hand him to her or risk dropping him.

"Wow! Ronan really likes you!"

Sine smiled and touched Ronan's nose with her nose. "That's because he knows I love him. I don't get to see him that often."

"All you need to do is ask, I will be happy to let you play with him more. In fact, I may ask you to take him a lot when the baby comes. I am sure Marcus will be helping, but two babies are going to become very demanding."

"Of course!" Sine said and her eyes danced with excitement. "I would love that!"

Shortly after Sine had gotten a warmer cloak, they began on their walk.

"Do you walk every day?" Sine asked.

"I try to, I don't always. It mostly depends on the weather. Today seemed like a perfect day. The sun is shining, and its air is crisp, but not windy. Perfect for walking."

As they walked, Sine and Moria talked about life in the castle and how different it was from living in the country.

"You know at first I was afraid I wouldn't like raising a child in the castle, but now I have grown to like it and even depend on it," Moria said. "Days that I am not feeling well I can simply ask for some help with Ronan. I never could have done that in my cottage. My nearest neighbor was a great help, but she was not extremely close. Besides, I don't think I ever would have gotten to know you. You have turned out to be one of my closest friends."

"Well, I think our friendship started when you practiced shooting with me," Sine said with a smile. "Funny thing, I have been working more and more with the sword, and it's so much more comfortable for me. Although I don't like the idea of hand to hand combat with some of these men, the bow just is tough for me to learn."

"I have heard Marcus tell his soldiers that during hand to hand combat, let their feelings fuel them. Perhaps that's something you should think about. If you're afraid, you won't be able to fight well, but if you're angry, I'm sure you would fight stronger."

"I haven't heard Marcus tell me that yet, but it does make a lot of sense. I sure have a lot of things to remember that would keep me angry at Dorcha and his men."

"As far as your archery skills, keep practicing. Sine, you are a good marksman, but with practice, you will get better. I really like shooting with the arrow. I can't imagine even holding the sword nevermind trying to fight with one," Moria said as she rolled her eyes, "Sine, what do you think of all this talk of war breaking out?"

Sine took in a deep breath and slowly exhaled. "I have been to the villages many times over the last few months. It seems that people's attitudes have changed. Most people get angry with me when I begin speaking about Cullen. Sometimes, they just abruptly walk away. I don't know what to make of it, but fighting sure feels imminent. Why do you ask?"

"It's probably just me, or maybe because now I have young children. I am honestly scared something might happen to Marcus. He tells me not to worry and reminds me that I have never been scared during any of the other battles he has fought. I just don't understand why this time I am nervous."

"It probably is because you have a young child and a new baby on the way. I'm sure Marcus is right, and you shouldn't be worrying yourself about it." Sine gave her an encouraging pat on her shoulder.

Moria doubled over in pain. "Oh," she cried, "I think the baby is coming!"

Sine tried not to panic. "What? You mean now? We are too far from the castle! What am I going to do! I can't leave you to go get help!"

Moria leaned heavily on Sines' shoulder and straightened slowly. After taking a few deep breaths, she said: "Sine, don't panic, I think I can walk for a little while, let's try to head back."

Moria had put most of her weight on Sine as they slowly began walking back to the castle. Ronan cried and stretched his hands out to his mother as if he knew something was wrong.

"It's okay Ronan," Sine said, "Mommy is going to be okay."

Sine wasn't sure if she was trying to convince Ronan or herself. Every few minutes, Moria had to stop walking to catch her breath as another wave of pain washed over her.

"Sine, This child is coming very fast, we are not going to make it to the castle," Moria said through clenched teeth.

Sine didn't want to help deliver the baby. "Moria, are you sure? I don't have any idea how to help!" Sine felt the fear rising up in her heart.

"Sine, I am a doctor. I will be able to talk you through it. I honestly don't ..." Moria stopped and let out a cry of pain. When the pain subsided, gasping for breath, she finished her sentence. "I don't feel like anything is going wrong. I need to sit down."

Sine helped Moria to a large rock that was near the road. She guided Moria around to the other side and said, "Sit here for a minute."

Sine knew it would be more than a minute, but she didn't know what else to say. Sine removed her cloak and laid it on the snow. "Here you go, boy," she said to Ronan as she placed Ronan on it. At least now Moria had a little privacy if a traveler should come down the road.

Sine felt helpless as the hours ticked by. Ronan began crying Sine didn't know if he was hungry, tired, scared or cold. All she could do was hold him and try to calm him down. The night was falling, and Sine did not like the idea of being outside the castle walls with a mother in labor and a young child in the dark of night. Moria seemed to be doing well, but each time the pain came, Sine wished she was closer to home.

"Sine," Moria's voice was barely a whisper. "I think the baby is coming now."

Sine felt her mouth go dry and her hands trembled. "Moria what am I supposed to do?!" She set Ronan on her cloak as he continued to cry "Sorry, buddy. Your Mommy needs me now."

Before Moria could answer Sine heard a call from the road.

"Moria!"

Sine's heart leaped! She knew that voice anywhere."Marcus! Over here! Oh, thank goodness your here!" Turning to Moria, she said, "Moria, Marcus found us!" Just then Moria let out another cry this time she began to push to help the child be born.

Marcus dismounted his horse as it was still running towards them. Running the last few feet to be by Moria's side."Moria! I'm here!"

Within minutes, the baby came. A loud cry from the little girl confirmed that she was alive and full of breath. Marcus had removed his cloak for Sine to use as a blanket for the baby. Wrapping the little girl tightly in Marcus' cloak, she handed the baby to Moria.

"Hannah. Her name will be Hannah," Moria said, "Isn't she beautiful?"

"More beautiful than any child I have ever seen," Marcus replied, as he kissed Moria on the top of her head, "Moria, what were you doing walking so close to the time the baby would come? When I came home for dinner, and you and Ronan were not there, I asked the maids. They said you went out walking this afternoon! I have never been so scared in my life! I had been searching for hours! Thank goodness for Ronan. His cry is how I found you."

"I had Sine with me, I was alright."

Sine looked up. "Well, I certainly didn't feel alright. That was not fun! I am so glad you came when you did Marcus."

Marcus was still visibly shaken. "Well, darkness is falling fast, let's get you and your children home." Turning to Sine, he said "Thank you for your help. Do you think you can carry Ronan and Hannah back to the castle? I will carry Moria, the horse will follow."

"Marcus, do you think you can carry her that far? I know we are still a good distance."

Marcus looked down at Moria, "I'm not sure, but I have to try. I will probably stop frequently to rest, but I am not giving up until Moria is safe."

Moria protested, "Marcus, you can't carry me! I will try to walk."

"Now, that's out of the question!" Marcus said with a very stern voice. "I am not giving you an option. I am carrying you!"

Sine had never heard Marcus angry before. There was no questioning he was upset. Moria did not try to argue. Sine knew not to say another word, but she was worried Marcus was trying to do too much.

Being in the woods after dark reminded Sine how she used to be so afraid of the woods. Meeting Cullen and Marcus had really changed her. Now she was no longer fearful, just alert. When Moria asked Sine to come for a walk earlier that afternoon, Sine almost left her sword at home. As she was walking out of her room, she decided to take the sword with her just in case. Marcus and Cullen had both told her they didn't want her to ever be without a weapon to defend herself.

They had been walking for what seemed like hours to Sine. Every few minutes they stopped to rest. Her arms were burning as she held the two children. Ronan had fallen asleep and was leaning precariously off her right shoulder. Hannah was such a fragile bundle, Sine was afraid to adjust either of them, but she couldn't help it. Sine knelt on the ground and gently lowered the two children onto the snow. She shook her arms to get the feeling back in them. First, she picked up Hannah and placed her in the crook of her left arm, then she scooped Ronan up in her right and leaned his body against her shoulder.

"Are you alright?" Marcus asked.

"Yes, my arms were going numb, but I will be fine. How are you holding up?"

Marcus gave a little laugh, "Well, I can't feel my arms either, and my back is very sore and tired, but ..." Looking down at Moria as she slept in Marcus's arms. "I have the most valuable bundle in my arms." Marcus tipped his head in an upward fashion as if he was trying to point upwards "I think I can make it."

Sine looked up in the direction Marcus was looking, there was the castle. *Why didn't I see how close we were before?* She wondered. Looking at the castle in the evening brought back the memory of the first night she called this place home. *Cullen, It's been over a year. How I miss you!*

Invaders

Nine months passed since Sine began her lessons with the bow and the sword. Marcus was increasingly confident that she would be able to hold her own if fighting ever broke out.

"You know, I think you have become one of my finest warriors, Sine."

Sine, who had been dueling with Patrick during practice, was barely out of breath. "Well, I couldn't have gotten this far without your patience and guidance." She smiled, "I remember at the beginning; I complained a lot about how tired I was and how much I felt like a failure. Between Moria and you, I gained enough confidence to try harder, and the more I worked, the better I became. Thank You."

Marcus remembered those conversations and gave her a sheepish smile as he nodded. "Yes, I remember, you sure tried my patience as well," he said with a chuckle. "Remember how hard it was for you to learn the bow? Now you never miss, and you shoot farther than most good marksmen I know. I must say, Cullen was right about you, he knew you would make a great warrior."

Marcus, hesitated as he seemed deep in thought for a moment. "Sine, I know Cullen asked you to go to the villages, be warned things are not as friendly out there as they used to be. Especially in the village of Neamhreireacht. If you want to go there, I want you to have someone with you. Is that understood?"

Marcus' orders caught Sine by surprise. "What are you saying?"

"I am simply saying to take a soldier with you or I will go with you myself. You are not to go alone."

"Why have things changed?" Sine knew the reason, but for reasons unknown to her, she wanted to hear Marcus explain it to her again.

"Sine, you know what is going on, why do you seem surprised? Cullen told us this was going to happen. He already knew that the people of Chrioch Olc would try to settle in the villages and create division within the kingdom. Well, it's been happening for a little while now, but just recently fights have begun to break out among the villagers."

"Can't we send the settlers away? Wouldn't that stop the problem?"

"Cullen doesn't want the settlers to be sent away. You see, many villagers from Chrioch Olc are begging for a chance to get away from King Dorcha. Cullen wants to give them a chance to show if they are loyal to him, he will take care of them as his own people. If they remain loyal to King Dorcha, it will be evident. That's a big reason for Cullen asking you to befriend the people in the villages. Cullen is a very compassionate man and doesn't want innocent people judged as bad just because they live in Chrioch Olc."

"So why are people fighting?"

"Not everyone in the villages is loyal to Cullen. We have our villagers who never really cared about King Cullen, and they are being influenced by the villagers who are coming in from Chrioch Olc and are genuinely loyal to King Dorcha. Then we have the people in the village who are very loyal to King Cullen and are angry with those who are speaking badly about Cullen. Tension is mounting in the village, and small fights are breaking out regularly. I have a squadron of soldiers stationed there to keep the fighting at a minimum."

"Well then, it sounds like just the village I should go visit," Sine said as she lifted her chin slightly in the air. "I can't just sit back and watch as someone speaks badly about Cullen."

Marcus was concerned. Didn't he just tell her she should not go there because it was dangerous? "If you want to go, then I will go with you. You are not to go alone. Change into villagers' clothes I don't want anyone to recognize who we are. We will leave in an hour."

Sine was nervous and excited at the same time. What was it about this trip that made her nervous? Since Cullen has been gone, Sine had made many trips into the villages as he asked. Some of those trips she enjoyed as she spoke with the people, but other times she met people who would ridicule her because of her love for Cullen. More and more people were dishonoring Cullen, and it was harder to find people who were still loyal. Most of the time, they were just irritated with her for talking about the king, but now she felt as if the irritation was something more.

Sine did as Marcus requested and dressed as an ordinary villager. As she turned and saw her reflection, she thought, *why do people dislike Cullen? After all the things that he has done for them? It's like they forgot who he is or all the things he has done to help them.* She remembered how full the great throne room was. Many people stood shoulder to shoulder asking for help and guidance. *How many actually wanted to know Cullen and how many just wanted a free hand out?* She wondered. Sadly, she realized that most of the people only wanted to get something from the king, but not really get to know him. Now that he had been gone for over a year, most people felt betrayed and blamed Cullen for things that were happening in their own life only because he wasn't giving them what they wanted.

Cullen, she thought, *Cullen, I know you're busy I know you're coming back, you promised me that you were, but I feel so lonely.*

Why are you lonely?

Sine took a deep breath. *Well, maybe it's because I wish you were here.*

Isn't Marcus and Moria still with you?

Yes, she thought. *But it's the people, they are losing their loyalty to you every day.* Sine's comment was only met with silence from Cullen. *I'm sorry Cullen,* she said, *I didn't mean to upset you.*

You didn't tell me anything I already did not know.

Sine could sense the sadness in his words. *I knew that people would lose their loyalty to me and turn against me. I was hoping that would not happen, but you confirmed it. Tell me, are there still people who are loyal to me?*

Oh yes! Many people are very loyal. In fact, there have been little fights starting in the village of Neamhreireacht. Your faithful men are getting angry with the villagers who are sowing discord.

I will be returning soon, do not lose heart.

Discord

Hannah was now three months old, and Moria needed to get out of the castle. When she heard Marcus tell Moria they were going to the village, Moria begged Marcus to let her come along. Moria left Ronan with one of the maids. Hannah was still too young to be without her mother for more than a few hours, so she strapped Hannah to her back.

As Sine, Moria, and Marcus approached the village, everything appeared peaceful. Once in the marketplace area, Sine was looking around for some of Marcus' men.

"Marcus, I thought you said you had men here to keep the peace?"

"I do!" he motioned in the direction of the merchants, "There is the captain now."

Sine realized that all the men were dressed like villagers, living like the people in the village and not showing their exact role there in the marketplace.

After spending several hours in the village with Moria and Marcus, Sine began to think her nervousness was not necessary. She observed the children playing and the women selling their ware in the market. As she strolled through the streets throughout the day, she had spoken with several people. Most of the people listened to her with disinterest, but not anger. A few young children loved hearing the stories of King Cullen and wanted to know more. Satisfied with the day's trip, she turned toward Marcus.

"Well, I guess we should head back now," she said.

"All right," Marcus replied, "just let me speak with Flannery before I leave."

As they headed toward Flannery's house, angry shouts could be heard. Marcus began to run toward the shouting as Moria and Sine did their best to keep up.

Since they were dressing as ordinary villagers, Sine figured that a bow slung over her shoulder would not be a good idea. Instead, Sine kept her sword with her under her cloak. She was hoping that she would not need to use it, but after Marcus' concern about a fight breaking out, she decided to be prepared. As they approached Flannery's house, it became evident that a fight had broken out. Many people were standing around shouting and cheering their favorite warrior on. Marcus pushed his way through the crowd of people just in time to see Flannery draw his sword.

"I am loyal to King Cullen," he said in a low voice that was challenging to the man who was fighting with him. Flannery looked very calm as he faced his opponent who now drew his sword.

"I have been given authority to kill all who remain loyal to Cullen!" Shouted the other man as he lunged forward at Flannery.

Lunging forward, his arms were raised leaving his sides wide open to get hit. Flannery swung his sword sideways and immediately hit his mark. The man let out a cry of pain as he fell to his knees. Flannery still holding his sword directly in front of the man's face as he said,

"I should have finished you off just then, but I have orders to capture you, not kill you."

The man laughed a cruel laugh. "Face it; you just don't have the heart to kill a person," he sneered.

"No," Flannery said, "I just follow orders."

Flannery turned to get the rope to tie the man up when people let out a gasp. Flannery turned just in time to see the man fall on his own sword and kill himself.

"Coward," Flannery mumbled under his breath.

Sine noticed the tension in the crowd was growing. People

were arguing among themselves about what had just happened. A thunderous voice shouted near her.

"You! You're the woman Cullen plans on marrying! My friend and I have been given authority to kill all of you. I will get a great reward for killing the bride!"

She turned to look at the man who was standing next to her. In one sudden movement, the man drew his dagger and swung at Sine. Suddenly she felt a sharp pain in her side. She pulled her sword from its sheath not even confident that she was now strong enough to hold it. Sine looked at the man who was now facing her. Sine immediately drew her sword and began fighting. She was surprised at the strength that she had. The wound on her side was hindering her fighting abilities but not as badly as she thought they would.

Marcus heard a young child crying.

"Hannah!"

He turned to see Hannah strapped to Moria's back screaming in fear as Moria was engaged in a fight. Marcus immediately came to her aid.

"Go home! Get Hannah out of the fighting. Tell Kelly we need assistance." Moria hesitated for a moment, turning, she ran as fast as she could toward Dia Richoet.

Hannah was still screaming as she ran down the road.

"Sorry Hannah, I cannot stop and comfort you right now."

Once within the castle gates, Hannah's cry brought people out to see what was happening. *Perfect* Moria thought, *Hopefully Kelly will come out knowing that Marcus is not here.* Sure enough, Moria looked up and saw Kelly running toward her.

Now with the entire army engaged in battle, it appeared that the whole kingdom was fighting, not just the village of Neamhreireacht. Night had fallen, but the struggle continued. Many of Cullen's men were wounded. Sine felt like they were outnumbered three to one.

Every time she finished fighting one soldier, another one challenged her. How long would her strength hold? Off in the distance, Marcus saw Sine struggling. She was looking rather tired. Once he defeated the soldier who was fighting with him, he made his way to fights alongside Sine.

"Sine," Marcus said as he motioned toward a nearby house, "we need to make our way toward that house. There we can have extra protection from the wall of the house."

Slowly, both Sine and Marcus walk toward the house as they continue fighting the men. Once they reached the house, they stood side by side with the wall of the house against their back. In the midst of the fighting, Marcus mortally wounded the man he was fighting.

"Sine, rest for a moment." Marcus began fighting the other man who had been engaging Sine in a sword fight.

Cullen Returns

Cullen had waited so long for this day. Side by side with his father they had prepared the perfect place for Sine. *I can't wait to see her expression when she sees Naofa Neamh.* He would often think as he worked. Cullen remembered the day his father called him aside to speak with him. 'Cullen, things are finally ready. Your house is already supplied with every good thing that you can offer your bride. Go and get her! Let the marriage feast begin!'

As Cullen traveled with his father's army, he thought about Dia Richoet. How was Marcus managing all his new responsibilities? How many people had lost their loyalty? He was sure that by now King Dorcha had begun a war among his people. The last time he spoke with Sine, she told him that fights were breaking out in the villages. He turned and surveyed the army that he was leading. The number of foot soldiers was so vast; they could not be numbered. They marched shoulder to shoulder with their armor gleaming in the sun. The captains rode upon white horses ahead of the men. Each man carried a special pouch filled with manna made from the flour of a leigheas plant. This manna had fantastic healing properties. If a warrior were wounded in battle, just a small bite of this manna and they would be healed and strengthened.

As he approached the Dia Richoet, he immediately saw people were already engaged in combat. Spurring the horse on, the army raced into the thickest part of the battle. Cullen directed his horse to the little village of Neamhreireacht. That's probably where the fighting started. Maybe he would find Marcus or Sine there. The ground shook from the urgency of the foot soldiers rushing into battle. The sounds of swords clashing together were in unison with the sounds of men shouting as they engaged in combat. Off in the distant, Cullen saw Sine resting against the wall of a house while Marcus was trying to fight off several men at once. He knew she must be tired, but now was not the time to rest.

As dawn broke, Sine leaned up against the wall of the house. *Oh, when will this ever stop?* She thought. *I can't last much longer.* Slowly she sank to the ground to sit. A second man joined in the fight against Marcus, and Sine was just about to get up to help when she noticed the earth was trembling.

Sine, I am coming!

Excitedly, Sine jumped to her feet and shouted,

"He's coming! Cullen is returning!"

Both men who were fighting Marcus glanced nervously over their shoulder to look for Cullen. Marcus took full advantage of the distraction and ran one of the soldiers through with his sword.

On the horizon, the very ground shook from the thunderous hooves of King Domnall's cavalry. Heading the cavalry was King Cullen. Behind the cavalry was an army so vast they could not be numbered. Their war cry was heard throughout the entire battlefield. It was such a thunderous sound it was deafening. It reminded Sine of the sound of a rushing waterfall. Sine took in the scene. The number of horses and the footmen that followed them covered the entire land. The pastures that were once green, now looked alive, flowing with movement. Men marched shoulder to shoulder coming across the meadows, like water flowing over the land, rushing to battle with urgency and excitement.

Sine heard Cullen's words as if he was by her side even though he was still on the horizon with his father's army. *Stand and fight!*

Sine noticed more of King Dorcha's men were coming toward them eager to fight. *I cannot stand any longer,* Sine thought.

Sine, you must stand your ground and fight!

The urgency in Cullen's voice prompted Sine to stand to her feet but she wasn't sure how much longer she would last, she was determined to fight her hardest even if it was to the bitter end. Visions of Philip filled her mind. He was so full of anger and hatred. She remembered all the hurtful things he did and said to her, the way he delighted in punishing both Cullen and herself. Those memories made a new kind of strength rise from within her. She turned to face the soldier that had just drawn his sword to fight with her. She found herself staring into eyes, filled with as much bitterness and hatred as Philip's.

The Great Battle

As the fighting continued, Sine heard faint sobs from within the house. Apparently one of the King Dorcha's men did, too. A large burly man disappeared into the house. Moments later he emerged with a young boy whimpering in fear and pain from the soldier's firm grasp on his arm. The soldier laughed a chilling laugh.

"Come to me, and I'll let this kid go free." His eyes were challenging her, and his smile was mocking her. The man continued. "Come on, I have heard you actually care about people. Surely this young child will compel you to act."

A few of nearby men had lowered their swords and began joining in with the mockery and laughter. "Save the little boy." They taunted her.

"Sine, No!" Marcus shouted.

Marcus could see the boy and the terrified look in his eyes. Immediately, he recognized Peter, the young boy who had almost been kidnapped two years ago. Peter had saved Marcus's life. If Sine knew that, she would do whatever she could to let the boy go free.

Sine looked directly at the young boy. His face was covered with dirt, but Sine could still see the freckles that played across each cheek on his fair skin where the tears had washed the soil away. His large green eyes were pleading with her for help. The soldier had his arms pinned behind his back which apparently gave him great pain.

"Let him go!" Sine said with determination, but her reply was only a roar of laughter from the men.

Suddenly, the young boy let out a cry of pain as the soldier roughly pushed him to the other soldier and took one step toward Sine.

"Make me!" he shouted in her face. "I told you I would let him go if you just came with me. How hard can that be?" Again, he laughed.

"Sine! Don't!" Marcus' voice was urgent as if he knew what Sine was thinking. "Sine, he will only kill both you and the child," he shouted.

Just then, an arrow shot through the air and pierced through the leather armor of the soldier who was closest to Sine. Startled at seeing his fellow soldier fall, the second soldier released his grasp on the boy's arm.

After the boy bolted free from the man's grasp, he ran to hide behind Marcus. A second arrow screamed through the air and the second soldier fell to the ground with a cry of pain. Sine turned to see where those arrows had come from. A distance away, there on his horse, was Cullen. Cullen dismounted the horse and ran through the crowds of warriors to be by her side. Once he was next to Sine, he untied a small pouch from his belt.

"Here, eat this bread. It will give you strength." Cullen turned to fight the men who were coming toward them to fight.

The bread was a flat, wafer-like, cracker. It tasted sweet and salty at the same time. Almost immediately Sine felt a new kind of strength rise from with her. She felt as if she was no longer fighting with her physical strength but more from her mental strength. She no longer felt the pain from the wound she had on her side. The exhaustion and hunger were gone and replaced with boldness and determination to defeat the one who tried so hard to beat her.

Sine stood to her feet, drew her sword and approached Marcus. "Here, eat," she said as she began fighting in place of Marcus. The soldier was a powerful and skillful fighter who would have easily destroyed Sine if she was still weak and tired but because of her renewed strength, she was able to defeat him quickly.

Now, for a brief moment, the three of them were free to talk. Cullen took the small pouch and fastened it back onto his belt as he said, "Come with me; we must find King Dorcha and defeat him. Then his men will flee fearing complete and utter defeat."

Sine turned towards Peter who was visibly shaken, hiding in the corner of the house. "What about this child, surely you won't leave him here alone in the heat of battle."

Marcus spoke up "My lord, please grant permission for me to get him to safety first. I will join you immediately once he is in a safe place."

Cullen nodded to Marcus. "Go, do as you have requested."

Sine followed Cullen to a pair of war horses ready for battle. They eagerly stomped the ground with their hooves and snorted the air, willing and eager for action. Sine and Cullen easily and swiftly mounted their horses. Once on the horse, Sine could see the fighting clearer.

So, this is why kings ride in battle, she thought.

"Yes," Cullen replied, "From this view, I can guide my warriors to victory."

Distinguishing between the armies was easy. King Dorcha's men looked dark and angry. Bitterness seemed to spill from their eyes. Some of them almost appeared animal-like, snarling and hissing at their enemies. They fought alone and with many different types of weapons. Some looked handmade, and others were already broken. Sine could tell which ones Cullen's men were, most of them wore their regular everyday clothes. They had been working and living out their normal everyday lives when the war began. During their training, they were taught to always put on the King's armor for protection under their regular attire and keep a sword with them at all times.

King Domnall's army was entirely different. They were dressed in dazzling white garments that showed through the open places in their armor. The armor was polished so perfectly it nearly blinded you if you looked at it. Undoubtedly that was one of the advantages that these men used. Each man stood tall and strong as if they were as proud as a young boy just beginning to fight. Every man carried a shield, sword and the same small pouch Cullen had tied to his belt.

The part that stood out to Sine the most was the way King Domnall's soldiers treated each other. They engaged in battle as a team. Two men are fighting together at all times. They never left one behind; if they saw one of Cullen's men fighting alone, they joined to help. Sine glanced in the other direction, and everywhere she looked she saw the same compassion for each other on the battlefield. Sine noticed some of King Domnall's men feeding small pieces of bread to the injured. As she watched, the wounded men stood looking strong again ready to fight all the harder.

Sine noticed that battle looked more intense off to the right side of the village. Cullen saw it too; he began guiding his horse through the warriors toward the fighting. As they approached, Sine could see King Dorcha and Philip. Just the sight of Philip made her stomach turn. Cullen did not turn his head to look at Sine but spoke directly to her heart.

"King Dorcha is for me to defeat, but your battle lies with Philip." Sine felt terror rise in her heart for a moment.

"Sine, do not fear, Philip's strongest weapons are his lies. Don't listen to them; they will tear you down and make you doubt yourself. The weapons of our warfare are mighty, and so are you. Remember, you are more than a conqueror. Philip tried to destroy you once, but he failed. Now, you will have complete victory over him. He knows he has already been defeated. When he takes one look at you, fear will grip his heart."

Again, the memories filled Sine's mind. She could feel the cold stone of the dungeon pressed against her back. She could practically smell the musty, dirty floor of the cell she spent so much time in. The way Philip laughed whenever she cried out in pain from his flogging.

Cullen's voice filled her mind. *Let those emotions give you strength and determination. Be strong and of good courage. Fear not, nor be afraid of Philip. I am with you, I will not fail you or forsake you. We will be victorious.*

Conquered

Cullen heard Sine's thoughts as she remembered the treatment that Philip had given her. He understood her fear but, he knew that she would conquer Philip; he had no doubt. Sine had become an excellent warrior with both the bow and the sword. Marcus had turned his fearful bride into a confident, strong warrior who did not seem to be afraid of anything. *Marcus, you did well.* Cullen thought to himself. Now, he needed to turn his attention to Dorcha.

Dorcha was not hard to find amid the fighting; he was seated high on his horse shouting out commands to the men that were fighting for him.

"Dorcha!" Cullen yelled.

Immediately Dorcha turned to see Cullen.

"Finally!" Dorcha gave a hearty laugh. "Now this time I will make sure I kill you for good!"

Even though he was mocking Cullen, Cullen could see the fear on his face.

"No, Dorcha, this is the end for you and all who follow you."

Terror gripped Dorcha's heart as he saw the authority emanating from Cullen's eyes. He jumped from his horse and began to run. Cullen glanced at Sine; she was engaged in a sword fight with Philip. She looked like she had the upper hand and Philip was tiring quickly.

"Dorcha!" Cullen shouted as he dismounted his horse and ran after him. "Don't be a coward, fight me!"

It did not take long for Cullen to catch up with Dorcha since he was a well-trained warrior. Dorcha turned to fight him this time the look of fear was evident on his face.

Even though Dorcha was filled with fear, he was still a good fighter. Cullen and Dorcha fought long and hard in a fierce sword fight. Cullen remembered the day in the safe haven with Sine when he put the healing balm on her wounds. Dorcha was going to pay for all the horrible things he did and said to Sine, his beloved. Cullen remembered the way Sine thought she was worthless because of Philip's constant belittling. He remembered the fear that she was now facing as she fought Phillip. His strength grew as he thought about Sine. Suddenly Dorcha made a sweeping motion with his sword that left him wide open for attack. Cullen quickly thrust his sword into Dorcha's chest.

As Dorcha fell, a cry went out among the soldiers who were near enough to see their king's defeat.

"Dorcha's dead! Retreat!"

Hearing the shouts that Dorcha had been killed, Philip turned to run. Sine was not a fast runner and knew that she would never catch up to Philip, so, she took a bow and arrow from a fallen soldier. *Steady,* she told herself. Sine took a deep breath and let it out slowly focusing on Philips' fast retreating back. After releasing the arrow, she watched it hit its mark. Philip tumbled to the ground and did not move again. Sine noticed Cullen was standing just feet from where Philip had fallen.

Excellent aim! He will never hurt you again.

Sine felt as if the world was moving in slow motion. She saw Marcus off in the distance chasing men as they began to retreat. To her right, Cullen was engaged in another fight. Confusion was taking over Dorcha's men. The fighting became more chaotic as men who were fighting were now trying to run the other way. Sine drew another arrow back in the bow aimed at the retreating, defeated army. Cullen shouted to his men.

"No Survivors! There are to be no survivors!"

At the sound of Cullen's command, a great war cry rose from the mouths of all of Cullen's men along with King Domnall's men. Cullen's vast army pursued Dorcha's men all the way to the forest. Not one of Dorcha's men was spared.

The Marriage Feast

That evening as they celebrated the victory over King Dorcha they enjoyed a great feast. Only those who had remained loyal to Cullen were allowed into the celebration. All the others were cast outside the castle walls. There was much remorseful crying as they realized what they had done. After the feast, Cullen got to spend time with Sine alone in the bridal chambers. Holding her in a firm embrace, he said, "Sine, oh how I have missed you. It's been so long. I've ached to just hold you again." He gently caressed her face as she spoke. "Sine, you are my greatest treasure. Do you realize that?"

"I have missed you terribly, also," her voice barely a whisper. She closed her eyes and drank in the sweet musky scent that was on his clothing.

"You do realize; we have already been married."

Sine was surprised. "What? When? I thought I was just waiting for you ..."

Cullen smiled. "Sine, you just didn't realize our customs. We were officially married when I wrote down my plans to marry you. That is a covenant I cannot break. At that time, I married you. I swore to you I would return, and here I am."

Sine remembered the day he wrote down his plans and posted them on the wall. She didn't understand why he had done that and she had dismissed the importance of it.

"Cullen, I am sorry I didn't realize ..."

Again, Cullen smiled. I knew you were unaware of our customs. I was not offended. But now that I am here, you understand that the place I have prepared for you in Naofa Neamh is finally ready. It took longer than you wanted, but it had to be perfect. Once It was finished, my father gave me the permission to return to get you. Tonight, we will consummate our love. Tomorrow, I will rejoice as I bring you to meet my father.

That night, finally being with Cullen, Sine surrendered to his loving caress. Nothing in the world would ever take her love away from him. Ecstatic joy flooded her soul, heart, and mind as she willingly gave herself to him.

Morning came, and Cullen quickly announced the plans to travel to King Domnall. Only Cullen's loyal subject was allowed to follow in the procession. They loaded many horses and donkeys with gifts of gold and precious treasures to offer the king. The excitement was in the air.

As they began the journey, the people started to singing praises to King Cullen and Domnall. Marcus was beaming with pride. He looked almost as happy as Cullen did. Sine had since realized the importance of Marcus. Cullen had entrusted Sine to his care for much more than a simple task. Marcus took this responsibility as seriously as if he was protecting the king himself.

The procession was so long it stretched on as far as the eye could see. The journey was long, but it felt as if it had only been a short time when Sine noticed a large city on a hill that seemed to beam in its own light. Cullen had ridden up next to her.

"Beautiful, isn't it?"

"It looks as if the light is coming from it," she said is a quiet voice that was filled with awe.

"Well, that's because it is. I can't tell you all my secrets, right now. We can explore all the mysteries of the kingdom together now that you are home. Let me just say that this light will never go out."

The closer they got to the city, Sine noticed a crystal clear, blue lagoon. Many of Cullen's soldiers and villagers were wading into the water and excitedly shouting.

"What is that?" asked Sine as she pointed toward the waters.

The beauty of the lagoon mesmerized Sine. The color looked as if it matched Cullen's eyes exactly.

"This place is called the Springs of Cura," Cullen said. "It is known for its healing properties. I have commanded all those who still had wounds from the battle to wade into the water to be healed and strengthened. Now, it's your turn."

Sine turned and looked at him. "My turn? I am fine!"

"Sine, you still have the wound in your side from fighting, and I know you still carry wounds from your previous time in Dorcha's grasp."

Cullen stopped Hunter and dismounted, reaching his hands toward Sine. She willingly obeyed and slid off her horse into his arms. Cullen picked her up and carried her into the pool.

"Honestly, I can walk myself," Sine said, but Cullen did not answer. As Cullen walked her deep into the water, fear began to creep into her mind. *Why isn't he talking to me and why is he walking me out to the deeper water?* She looked around and noticed that all the other people had stayed in the shallow water.

"I can feel your fear. What is the matter?"

"Why are you going so deep?" Sine questioned.

"Because I like the deeper water, it's cooler, and the healing properties are stronger. I knew you would settle for the shallow water, that's why I am walking you out deeper."

Sine looked into Cullen's eyes, yes, they were the same color of these water. Sine was honestly surprised by the amount of peace that flooded her soul as she looked into his eyes.

"I trust you," she said with a smile. "Isn't that what you have wanted to hear?"

Cullen smiled, and his eyes sparkled. "Yes, I've been waiting a long time to hear that knowing you honestly meant it. Now, hold your breath, I am going to put you into the water now."

As Cullen gently lowered her into the water, she could feel a hot tingling sensation on her side where her wound was. It was a strange sensation, but a comforting one. Cullen continued to lower her into the water until she was entirely under the water. The healing liquid washed over her entire body and peace filled her senses. As she relaxed in his arms, she felt heat surge through her body. Cullen had now lifted her up out of the water just enough that she could breathe but kept her body submerged under the healing water.

"Sine, I want you to think about all the people who had hurt you in the past like Philip and Dorcha. Forgive them for what they did to you and let the memories go. They will only beat you if you hold unforgiveness towards them. Sure, your past was hard, but you will no longer look back on the difficult times, but just remember the good times we had. You will no longer dwell on who hurt you but on how much you have changed."

As she remembered each hurtful thing, she cried and then tried her best to forgive. The heaviness in her chest was lifting. She knew Cullen was right. Cullen had released her legs into the water so she could stand on her own. Cullen embraced her, as she let the tears flow freely.

"Sine, I know it's not easy to forgive, but it is necessary."

Sine began to weep as the memories filled her mind. So many times, she had used those memories to protect herself or to get the strength to fight but now releasing them took considerable effort. Cullen continued to hold her in an embrace until her tears stopped.

"Now, let's finish our journey home," he said.

Sine's heart felt like it skipped a beat *home* she thought, *finally a place to call home.* Cullen turned and walked hand in hand with her back to her horse.

As they neared Naofa Neamh, Cullen's eyes shone with excitement. As soon as they entered the city, Cullen showed Sine a crystal-clear river.

"This river is called the River of Life. It flows right through the middle of the city."

Sine noticed the trees that grew along the river banks. The trees were vigorous and filled with different kinds of fruit that Sine had never seen before. Sine knew her mouth was gaped open as she looked around in wonder and amazement.

"Cullen!" Her voice barely a whisper, "It is beautiful!"

"Wait until you taste the fruit of those trees," he said, "I guarantee they taste sweeter than any fruit you have ever tasted. Come, you must meet my father!" Cullen said excitedly as he took her by the hand and lead her to the castle.

The castle shimmered like a precious gem, pulsating with light. The walls of the castle were majestic and high with twelve gates. The gates had precious gemstones and pearls embedded in them. There were three gates on the east side, three on the north, three on the south, and three on the west side. She saw guards posted at each entrance. The walls were made from pure jasper, and the floor was laden with gold so pure and hammered out that it looked translucent. Sine stopped Cullen just before he entered the throne room.

"How can this be? I could never have imagined a place like this!" Her eyes, brimming with tears of awe and wonder.

"Now this is your home; you will stay with me forever. You will never need or want anything, Sine." Gently, he wiped a stray tear that slipped down her cheek. "Now, we will have none of that," he said gently, "There shall be no tears here. I forbid it."

"Oh, Cullen!" again her voice was barely a whisper.

Cullen took her into his arms. "I told you I would prepare the perfect place for you. Now, instead of being shocked, enjoy it!" After a moment in an embrace, he stepped back and held her at an arms distance away. Looking deeply into her eyes, he said, "Are you ready to meet my father now?"

Sine swallowed hard. "Well, I am intimidated, but yes, I want to meet your father."

"Good, I can't wait to introduce you."

As they approached the throne room, the doors swung open by themselves. "Come in!" a deep voice boomed.

Sine felt herself tremble but knew she had nothing to fear. As they walked into the throne room, Sine had to squint against the bright light that illuminated the throne. Seven blazing fire torches were near the throne. The floor before the throne looked like clear crystal.

"Welcome Sine! I have been waiting to meet you, my dear."

Overwhelmed by respect of the majestic King, Sine fell prostrate on the floor before the throne. Cullen helped her to her feet.

"Sine, strength to your legs. There is no need to fear, you are my child."

Sine heard the words but had a hard time accepting them.

"A bride of my son is a daughter of mine. Welcome to the family."

Hours later, Cullen escorted Sine into a tremendous banqueting hall. The cheers were deafening as they entered the room.

"Long live King Domnall! Long Live Cullen and Sine!"

Dinner was served with the most exquisite foods Sine had ever seen or tasted. Laughter and joy filled the room while everyone celebrated. They celebrated for many days with joyful music and dancing. Sine had never experienced this kind of joyous celebration.

Now, this was her home. Cullen would never again leave her side, and no war would break out. They had defeated all their foes just as was foretold.

Dear Reader,

You have just read my story. I am Sine, the woman who had no idea why anyone would love me the way that Cullen loves me. I feared situations that were outside my control daily. Once I encountered Cullen's love for me, I had a difficult time accepting it or believing that it is real. Through Cullen's persistence, I realized that I need to see myself through the eyes of love. How did love see me? Let me tell you what I learned.

Cullen saw me through the eyes of pure love. He knew that I was helpless to get free from the chains that held me. Cullen knew that the only way I would be free is if someone paid the price for my freedom. When he thought of me, he did not see all my failures or problems, he only saw who I really was. A great warrior, and a beloved bride.

Jesus is like Cullen. He looks at you and me with that same kind of love. He knows that we are unable to get free from the sin that binds us fast to the wall in the devil's dungeon. Jesus came to rescue you from the prison of sin and set you free to a life of abundant freedom and joy. Just like Cullen, Jesus is a compassionate man who does not get angry with us when we doubt his love. He patiently waits for us to trust him. His passion is undying and beyond anything you or I can understand. Without his ultimate sacrifice, we would still be in bondage, unable to free ourselves from sin and the devil's hold. After he rose from the dead, Jesus tells us that the devil and his chains are powerless against us. The price has been paid for us, he reminds us every day that his love is unending. The prison door is left wide open, all we need to do is walk free. 'How do you do that?' You may be asking yourself.

Well, the first step is to accept that Jesus died for you when you were still a sinner. He loves you just as you are now. Don't worry about getting cleaned up for him. Thank him for the sacrifice that he made to set you free. Acknowledge him as your savior.

Next, simply talk to him! Talk to him like he's your best friend. He already knows everything about you, but he is longing to communicate with you. Then study the word that he has given us. Just as described in the Throne Room, God has given us instructions for our life situations. You need to read and obey the words to learn from him. The more you learn what he says about you, the more you will hear him speak to your heart.

If you have past hurts and unforgiveness, he has the healing balm that will heal you, and cleanse you if you give those wounds to him. Just like when I turned and let Cullen spread the ointment across my back. I was afraid that exposing my wounds would only make it worse. I believed that if I pretended the wounds were not there, no one would know. Jesus doesn't want us to act like the scars are not there, He wants to heal them. Open wounds are likely to become a deadly infection. It's the same with unforgiveness. When we don't forgive, it infects our entire life.

Realize that Jesus is in heaven with his father preparing a place for his bride. In the Bible, it is clearly written where Jesus tells us that he is going to go and prepare a place for us. Jesus also says that no man knows the day or the hour of his return, but he is returning to get his bride. He wants us strong to be able to ward off any attack that may come your way. The sword that I welded in my story is light and double-edged. The bible is often described as a double-edged sword. Study his words so you may be strong should the need ever arise where you need to put the "Philips" of your life away.

Glossary

Cullen – "Son of the Holy One – represents Jesus

Domnall – Ruler of the world – Represents God the Father

Dorcha – dark – stands for the devil

King Oscar and Queen Aideen – Sine's parents

Kingdom of Chrioch Olc – Start of Evil – King Dorcha's empire

Kingdom of Dia Riocht – God's Kingdom – Cullen's empire

Kingdom of Esperanza- Kingdom of Hope

Lugar Sombrío – Shadow place

Marcus – Rendered to mars, warlike – Represents the Holy Spirit

Moria – Rebellious woman – Marcus' wife

Mo'rmhuir Cathair– open sea city – King Luke's empire

Naofa Neamh – Holy heaven – King Domnall's empire

Nochtadh - Revelation

Philip – stands for our own personal struggles that beat us down daily and keep us captive to our own fears

Sine – God is Merciful - Cullen's bride - Represents the Bride of Christ.

The village of Neamhreireac – Village of Discord

Scripture references

Price of Freedom
- o Song of Solomon 8:16
- o Isaiah 26:4
- o Matthew 27:30
- o Isaiah 52:14
- o Isaiah 53:7
- o Hebrews 12:2
- o Song of Solomon 8:6

Healing Coming
- o Isaiah 61:10
- o Ephesians 3:18
- o Song of Solomon 4:9
- o Ephesians 3:18

Safe love
- o Song of Solomon 1:17
- o Song of Solomon 4:9
- o John 14:18
- o Exodus 19:5

Throne Room
- o 2 Chronicles 3:14
- o Hebrews 4:16
- o Romans 12:9
- o John 15:12

Winter is past
- o Song of Solomon 2:11-12
- o John 13:33-36
- o John 14:1-3
- o Hebrews 4:12
- o John 15:16

Be Alert
- o John 6:39
- o John 10:27-30
- o John 10:10

Goodbye
- o Song of Solomon 5:3-6
- o Matthew 24:36
- o Mark 13:32
- o Acts 1:11

Training
- o John 14:15
- o John 15:14

The Great Battle
- o Psalms 6:10
- o 2 Corinthians 10:4
- o Joshua 1:9
- o Isaiah 41:10

The Marriage Feast
- o Revelations 21:23
- o Revelation 22:1
- o Revelation 21:12,18
- o Revelation 21:4
- o Song of Solomon 2:4

Edwards Brothers Inc.
Ann Arbor MI. USA
May 2, 2018